TWO SPINSTERS AND A DUEL

EVE TARRINGTON

❧   I   ❦

I am sensible of the motions both of grace and passion and,
by turns, yield to each.
Heloise to Abelard, Letter V

"Judith!" Louisa-Margaretta said from the top of the
rocks. "If you insist on remaining cowardly and low, I
will eat our picnic before you arrive!"

Miss Louisa-Margaretta Haddington's horse had
reached the mountaintop so quickly that she had been forced
to stop short. With no particular interest, she sat comfortably
surveying the land her family had owned for only a season. It
was common knowledge that Wycliff Castle and its beautiful
grounds meant little to her. She was far prouder of her horse.
She made no move to remove the provisions her cook had so
carefully laid by.

Miss Judith St Clair, the rector's daughter, picked her way
up the rocks with a caution that indicated little faith in her
horse and perhaps even a deficit of faith in God.

"Are you determined to make me cross?" Judith called up,

glaring at Louisa-Margaretta. "I cannot go any faster. I'm already dizzy. I shall faint."

The sight of Louisa-Margaretta in her elegant riding habit, looking rather bored after conquering the peak, was not a welcome one for Judith.

"I thought you said that fainting was a ladylike but deceitful response to impossible situations." Louisa-Margaretta swung herself off the horse so easily it looked as if she were dismounting from a pony, not a headstrong mare.

"Well, this is impossible, for you are a tyrant," Judith said. "If one day you meet Napoleon Bonaparte, I daresay you two will have a great deal in common."

Louisa-Margaretta laughed. Her lack of concern about the Corsican was one of the things that drew Judith to her. Judith herself was terrified that Napoleon would lead an army into England, as promised, and that he would make Europe utterly unrecognizable if he succeeded. But Louisa-Margaretta was bored by political talk. Napoleon Bonaparte brought a hush or a drunken row to most every drawing room, but his name held no fascination for her.

"Napoleon Bonaparte is not the only tyrant," Louisa-Margaretta said as her friend made her way up the last bit of path then slumped in her seat, too exhausted to get off the horse. "Many of those colonists found our beloved king to be rather a tyrant too."

Judith frowned. "At least he took his office seriously," she said. "The prince of Wales is in great danger of making the most devoted monarchists lose their faith."

Louisa-Margaretta began taking out the food. "Enough politics. I don't care a jot about the prince of Wales. He's exactly the same as most of the young men I came up with, only he gets to rule an empire, more fool he. Tell me about your heart."

Judith stopped short. "My heart? It is very well, thank you."

"Nonsense, my idiot cousin broke it, and you haven't been a bit well since. You needn't scowl at me. At least I care enough to notice more than anyone else, perhaps excepting your sister."

Judith's sister, Miriam, in fact, had likely not paid much attention to the state of Judith's heart. Miriam herself was not in good spirits, especially since their aunt Leah had left the family to visit a cousin near their former home in the village of Brackenfield. Essex was a long journey away, and there was no telling when she would return to visit her nieces and nephews in Derbyshire. Miriam had begged to go on the picnic, and Louisa-Margaretta would not have refused her, but Judith hadn't allowed it. She was tired of quarreling with her sister and wanted an afternoon with only her friend. Judith could be as cross as she liked with Louisa-Margaretta, who refused to take offense.

"I'm not heartbroken," Judith said carefully. "I am not one of those delicate ladies who take to their beds at the slightest disappointment."

Louisa-Margaretta brought out a round of cheese and some fruit along with salmagundi, which had gotten tossed about horribly on the way up the mountain, then held Judith's horse as the latter inelegantly slumped over the saddle and tumbled to the ground far below.

"No," Louisa-Margaretta said. "But you write gloomy music on the pianoforte, and you scrub your father's church to within an inch of its life, and you refuse to do anything outside your own home."

"I risked my life to come on this picnic with you." Judith sat and delicately took one piece of egg from the salmagundi. It did not look particularly appetizing, but she needed something to occupy her hands.

"Any event where gentlemen might be present, I mean. Even though my parents are still trying to marry me off."

Judith frowned, looking into her friend's eyes for the first time. "What of your heartbreak, then, Louisa-Margaretta?"

"No. We are speaking of yours."

And indeed, Judith thought only of hers. While she remembered, somewhat vaguely, that Louisa-Margaretta had been disappointed in love, the details remained unclear to her. She had never met the young man, never had any involvement beyond sneaking a missive for him into one of the letters she wrote to an old friend of hers. Letty had posted the letter, and that had been the end of it. If Louisa-Margaretta's pride was hurt because she had never heard back from the gentleman, she did not tell Judith.

No, Judith was indeed thinking of her own heartbreak, in part because a particular confession had been given not far from where she sat.

It had been a winter afternoon, February, with hints of spring in the air. Mr Morgan Ramsbury praised Judith for her role in clearing up a murder for the Haddington family. She found that, much as she waved away the praise, she secretly revelled in it.

"You and my cousin Louisa-Margaretta were uncommonly clever," he said. "And you were so brave, Miss St Clair! If not for your actions, we might have never known there was any trouble at all. Louisa-Margaretta gives you all the credit, and I am inclined to agree with her."

"And what of your grief?" Judith asked quite sincerely, for the murder had torn his life apart for a time, and she was aware of the changes it had caused.

Mr Morgan Ramsbury had himself been accused of the murder, and Judith knew he was too sensible to forget that experience quickly.

"I am healing," he said. "In this new year, I have found a

purpose that might have been absent otherwise. And so, while I cannot be thankful for what happened, I can lay claim to some wisdom, I think."

Judith nodded thoughtfully. "I'm not sure that I could. Except the wisdom, perhaps, of not trusting first impressions."

"I can boast of having gained some wisdom in large part due to the blessing of your friendship, Miss St Clair," he said, and Judith coloured.

She did not dare reply, though she knew it to be true enough.

They walked in silence, remembering an exceedingly difficult and confusing time and also trying in vain to speak of the feelings that had become plain to both. Judith, still emerging from her grief after her mother's death, had been slow to recognize her feelings for Mr Ramsbury. Every time she watched him dancing with another lady, she felt cross, though for weeks she could not understand why.

"Louisa-Margaretta suspected you of being a murderer." Judith smiled, knowing that Mr Ramsbury still thought fondly of his cousin and had not been surprised that she had jumped to a rash conclusion.

"Of course! I do not have her confidence or her powers of speech, so naturally, she should feel my presence in her home somewhat strange."

"It was more than that, I think. She believed you were avoiding her mother." Judith looked at him, curious as to how he might receive the news.

"To be perfectly honest," he said, "I was avoiding my aunt. Or rather, both of my aunts. For different reasons."

"Your aunt Matilda because you found her vulgar." Judith knew it was forward, but equally, she was sure she could be quite honest. Mr Morgan Ramsbury had never yet been offended by her statements of fact, and they had already discussed his aunt Matilda at length in the first months of the year.

"I did not know what to make of her," he said. "We had rarely spent time together before she turned up. I was not comfortable, then, around nearly any of my family."

"And Mrs Haddington? Whyever would you wish to avoid Louisa-Margaretta's mother?"

He hesitated, giving Judith a chance to adjust her cloak. The day was a windy one, so despite the sun, she was cold, but she did not wish to go in. There, in sight of anyone who wished to see them from the grand house, she and Mr Morgan Ramsbury were in as secluded a spot as they could manage.

And as he turned red, Judith was struck with the need for a private *tête-à-tête*. Nobody who saw them could have guessed what they were talking of, though they might have seen Mr Ramsbury's steps slow and Miss St Clair's attention turn all at once to his exceedingly handsome face, its expression equal parts embarrassment and amiability.

"Miss St Clair," he said, "you have seen me through one of the most terrible times of my life. These months that I have known you should have held nothing but sadness, and yet, I feel a joy that I have never known with another."

She held her breath, knowing the question he would put to her and longing for it even as she dreaded the necessity of speaking.

"Before I speak plainly," he said, "I need to tell you something that, out of respect for my aunt, I have not shared with my family."

Her mind immediately fell to marriage then to bigamy. If he was speaking of respecting Mrs Haddington, the answer must be that he was engaged elsewhere, or worse, already married. He had come to spend Christmas with the Haddingtons in part because Louisa-Margaretta's parents were desperate to see her married off before she tried to make an unsuitable match, so they would want to pretend to the world that he was a bachelor. And Judith felt all the pain of her loss in that instant as well as the exquisite joy of hearing Mr Morgan Ramsbury declare his feelings. She knew, at last, that he had lingered for two months, not because London was unpleasant in the winter, but because he was in love with her.

"You are…" she began, but the words failed her.

"A nonconformist. Yes. I am."

Judith did not know whether to faint or run. Eventually, she sank into the snow, her eyes brimming with tears. "Mr Ramsbury," she said, "how could you keep this from me?"

When the memory struck her, Judith tried not to allow tears to fall, but it was in vain. Many months later, she still could not think of Mr Morgan Ramsbury's declaration without a fresh loss of hope. Louisa-Margaretta was ready with a handkerchief, one that was quite dry.

Judith St Clair buried her face in it. To see her, one might have thought that romantic sensibility was as great a source of shame as the murder that she and Louisa-Margaretta had examined so closely during their first Christmas together.

"How do you bear it?" Judith begged. "You are heartbroken, but you still ride, and you laugh. I cannot understand it."

Louisa-Margaretta, who was always hungry, took a most unladylike handful of salmagundi and passed a bit of carrot to her horse. "Being in love is divine. And to think, some never experience the emotion! Not all of us can marry where we love, but that is no reason not to live. If I am faithful to my beloved, I shall die happy."

"That is singular," Judith said. "I cannot think of dying happily, not if I am to feel this way my whole life."

"Heloise did," Louisa-Margaretta said. "Here, I brought this volume for you. Perhaps her thoughts will cheer you."

Judith frowned. "Did Heloise not resent her life as a nun and pine for her husband the whole time? Did she not feel angry at Abelard, and at her uncle, for the rest of her life?" She paused. "Does your mother know you have this volume?"

Louisa-Margaretta grinned wickedly. "It is very well hidden, dear Judith. I got Percival to buy it years ago. He is the only one of my brothers who is any fun, and he is to come visit us on Sunday! His regiment will be stationed nearby."

Judith started, wondering how any of Louisa-Margaretta's brothers had ended up in such a remote part of the country. They were all older than she was and all with similarly fanciful names. "What, your brother's regiment is coming all the way to Derbyshire? How did that come to be?"

Louisa-Margaretta, still chewing the food she had taken earlier, took a bite of a rather crushed currant cake. "Some machinations of my mother's, I am sure. She is probably sick of my company and would like one of her sons to amuse her. Percival pleased her by marrying, though unfortunately, he is still childless. I like his wife better than all my other sisters-in-law put together."

Judith had gone silent again, staring down over the hills and at the house below, remembering the man she had thought of as her Mr Ramsbury with more pain than pleasure.

Louisa-Margaretta jostled her arm, opening the book. "Listen to this passage. 'I will own to you what makes the greatest pleasure I have in my retirement: After having passed the day in thinking of you, full of the dear idea, I give myself up at night to sleep. Then it is that *Heloise*, who dares not without trembling think of you by day, who resigns herself entirely to the pleasure of hearing you and speaking to you. I see you, *Abelard*, and glut my eyes with the sight.

Sometimes you entertain me with the story of your secret troubles and grievances and create in me a sensible sorrow; sometimes forgetting the perpetual obstacles to our desires, you press me to make you happy, and I easily yield to your transports. Sleep gives you what your enemies' rage has deprived you of; and our souls, animated with the same passion, are sensible of the same pleasure.'"

Judith, who knew that "what your enemies' rage has deprived you of" referred to the fact that Abelard's enemies had castrated him, exclaimed aloud at that part of the passage, which Louisa-Margaretta read with great gusto. And at once, they fell backwards, laughing at the words and at each other.

For the first time since Mr Ramsbury had left, Judith's eyes filled with tears of mirth, not of sorrow. She turned to her friend, though, with a burning question. "You take Heloise, then, as your example that a woman can find pleasure in life after her heart has been broken? When still she is clearly miserable with longing?"

Louisa-Margaretta shut the book firmly. "Yes. Because how much more tragic would it be had she married another? Instead, by at least remaining faithful to her Abelard in her heart, she can keep her love alive forever."

Judith remained doubtful. "Would it not be difficult, though, to live one's whole life this way?"

"To be changeable in one's affections would surely be more difficult. Tell me, have you forgotten my cousin?"

Judith took a dainty bite of cucumber before squinting at the sun, which was lower than she had thought. She began to wrap up their small picnic, admiring the delicacy with which the Haddingtons' cook had parceled out their food, little imagining that Louisa-Margaretta's love of cantering would ruin the arrangement. "No, of course not."

"Well then, think of him, but also live. Tell me, when you

feared for your life ascending these rocks, did your misery not lessen?"

Judith smiled. "I suppose so. I felt as if I should fall from the saddle at any moment and break my head."

Louisa-Margaretta snatched the jam puffs before Judith could put them away. "Very well. I shall have a little card party when Percival is here, and you must come—with your sister, since you claim to be always quarreling with her. This gathering will delight her. Then she won't cause you any more trouble! Percival's friends may not be the most intelligent, but they always amuse me."

Judith shook her head. "My father dislikes cards, generally."

"Well, bring him, too, if you must. But it will be very proper and just the thing."

And with that, Louisa-Margaretta got to her feet, prepared to help her friend into what seemed an impossibly high and intricate saddle.

❧   3   ☙

When Judith finally arrived at the card party with her father and sister, she did not know how to give a reason for their lateness. For they had come far too late for any nonsense about horses or weather or even clocks to pass muster.

"My dears," their father said as they ascended the steps. "For all our sakes, you two will have to make peace."

"I am not the one who has to do anything," Miriam said. "Judith chose to pretend that her friend did not invite me."

"No, I said I was going, and you displayed such unbridled contempt that I—"

When the door opened, neither smiled, but they did fall silent, especially when they saw their hostess hurrying to greet them. She was a woman who loved to speak at the best of times, but she was too well-bred to scold them.

"Oh, the very dear St Clair family! Mr St Clair, I did not get to share half my thoughts on your brilliant sermon. I hope I may share them today. And Miss Miriam St Clair, how you have grown! Dear Miss St Clair, I am so glad you shall be here for Louisa-Margaretta and my daughter-in-law. We Haddingtons are used to having a great deal of gentlemen about, and yet, even I was longing for more feminine company! You are looking ever so well. Come see. Louisa-Margaretta's hair is a marvel. What a blessing to spend this pleasant evening together."

They were shown into a room where Louisa-Margaretta and a young woman who could only be her sister-in-law sat at a table, playing cards with two gentlemen. Other gentlemen had gathered by the fire, only one of whom looked cheerful. His wispy brown hair resembled his father's. He must be the younger Mr Percival Haddington. Judith herself had very similar hair, and she always pitied others who shared it. When one had so very little hair, not much could be done to make it look more appealing.

The description of Louisa-Margaretta's hair as "a marvel" had not been an exaggeration in any sense. Judith's friend had a massive amount of beautiful golden tresses arranged to perfection. Louisa-Margaretta, content in the knowledge that she was beautiful, did not generally care to trouble herself over the nuances of her toilette, and Judith wondered how a young woman buried in the country could look just as fashionable as any grand lady of the *haut ton*.

After Judith was introduced to Mr Percival Haddington, with his red face and warm smile, she met Mr Rollo Oakley, a man who looked as exceptionally well-groomed as Louisa-Margaretta, and the stiff and unfriendly Mr Honor Haskett. All three, apparently, were brother officers, though she quickly saw that they had little in common in terms of character.

She was distracted as they were introduced to the other officers, their colonel, and Mrs Peggy Haddington, Mr Percival Haddington's wife. It was interesting to see how different men might come together with a common aim, and she envied them their mission. Judith herself would hardly be permitted to leave the village unless she married, much less take up arms to defend England from Napoleon Bonaparte.

"How come you gentlemen to be here?" her father asked gently after the introductions came to an end. "Am I to understand that your regiment is here from Essex, our former home?"

"Why are we so far from France, you mean?" Mr Percival Haddington's eyes twinkled. "Well, can't have us all in one place, what? A disaster, that."

"We are not to discuss matters of strategy with civilians." Mr Honor Haskett was tall and thin, with hair so light it might have been grey. His face did not show any marks of age, and yet, his sour expression was that of a much older man.

Judith quickly perceived that he was one of those lucky fellows whose first name described him perfectly. She had previously observed the phenomenon only in women, such as her exceptionally kind friend Patience and a beauty she had once met named Rose. It was clear that Mr Haskett prized honor and propriety above many other things. Though he did not have the elegant looks of Mr Oakley, his uniform was brushed and polished so flawlessly that she wondered if he insisted on doing it himself.

"Come now," Mr Oakley said. "Mr Haddington is right. With everything in the broadsheets, who in the country does not know that Napoleon gathers his soldiers in one place, waiting for his moment to sail to England? Who is not aware that our regiments all prepare to defend the coastline or to go wherever else we might be needed? I am sure we need not be uneasy in such pleasant company. These elegant ladies will hardly betray our regiment's strategy to the French." He smiled at Judith and Miriam.

Miriam shifted beside Judith. Thinking of Mr Morgan

Ramsbury, Judith felt that she ought to be able to ignore Mr Oakley's smiles, but she was very aware of them nonetheless.

"We can certainly talk of other things," Judith said. "Are we all to play cards?"

It was as if she had spoken some kind of incantation. In a flash, Mrs Haddington was by her side again, all smiles and warm embraces.

"My dears, what a thrill to have all of you here and with my dear children! As soon as that little group finishes their game, I can promise we have something much better than cards. For my children, I said one game of cards, but not more! Since we are all here gathered with our dear rector, I thought we could play a game of a religious nature."

Judith glanced at her sister before she remembered their quarrel, and Miriam glanced back, her face reflecting Judith's despair at the gloomy prospect. Neither had forgotten how Mrs Haddington had decided to replace the "kissing ball" customary around Christmas with a "praying ball" of her own invention. She'd delighted in dragging her guests beneath the ball and insisting they pray aloud together, a task much more embarrassing than one kiss might have been.

"We will play charades, with the Bible as the theme," she said. "Easter, specifically, if we might prepare!"

Mrs Haddington got the card players away from the table. A large gentleman, who had been introduced to them as Colonel Chant, told her gently that they had all still been playing, but she took no notice.

"Yes, of course, my dear colonel," she said. "But I could not possibly ask the rector and his daughters to play cards, whereas writing charades, that is a different thing entirely. I cannot play myself, of course. I have written them all! Now, we will not have any acting here. Only I will put you in little groups so may let your wit flow."

Judith was in a pair with Mrs Peggy Haddington and Mr

Harcourt Green, a fellow officer. Though she was disappointed not to get a chance to speak with her friend, she soon forgot her troubles, as both Mr Green and the young Mrs Peggy Haddington seemed eager to include her in their merriment. They spoke with easy familiarity. Mr Green was exceptionally small and thin. His frame and his easy manners made him seem more like another Haddington relative than the rather terrifying figure he might have seemed had Judith encountered him on the battlefield.

Since Mrs Haddington did not wish them to act, they were to write a small poem on their given subject. The poem needed to convey both the larger idea and the specific words of the phrase, and they would win acclaim for wordplay and poetic imagery.

"True cross," the young Mrs Haddington groaned. "Oh dear. I do not see how we could possibly be witty on this subject, especially without offending the rector."

Judith ventured a little smile. "He is not easily offended."

"It is a grim topic, to be sure," Mr Green said with a much warmer smile. "But I shall take you at your word, Miss St Clair. I am sure we can find something unoffensive to our hostess, in any case."

She did not miss that Mrs Haddington had arranged the little circles with a nod to the practice of seating unmarried ladies with eligible gentlemen, while remaining careful that such pairs were not alone. Judith, for example, would have been quite cowed by Mr Green's handsome face and amiability had not the younger Mrs Haddington been with them. Miriam was seated with Mr Haskett but also with the elder Mr Haddington, and Louisa-Margaretta was with her brother and Mr Oakley. The hostess herself went between groups, returning to the rector every so often to give a lyrical commentary on his sermon of the previous Sunday. The rector sat with Colonel Chant, who looked rather bored.

Mrs Haddington also insisted that her guests help themselves to refreshments. Judith tried to take a ladylike portion, though she was surprised to find herself rather hungry for the first time in recent memory. Even if she would never have Louisa-Margaretta's appetite, perhaps she could keep herself from returning to the gaunt looks that had plagued her last Christmas. She remembered with sadness that she had found it easier to eat and smile, and even to cry, when Mr Ramsbury had been near. Since his departure, she had begun, once again, to eat only the little that she needed to stay awake and avoid pains in her stomach.

It helped that the Haddingtons had a wonderful cook. Judith noticed that the wine must have been rather excellent too. Mr Green took very little, but the rest of the gentlemen drank one glass after another.

After Judith took a few bites, she felt more herself and returned to the task of composing a charade. She, the young Mrs Haddington, and the amiable officer had made next to no progress. They had thought of nothing for the first two lines beyond Mr Green's mild suggestion that they might use the navigational meaning of the word "true" to make the whole thing cleverer.

"I have the last two lines, then," Mrs Peggy Haddington said. "Together, something valuable, though it is long since gone. The Papists think they've bought it, though of course, they're wrong."

Mr Green tittered. "I'm sure that would not do, would it, Miss St Clair?"

Judith started. "I'm sorry. Well, I'm not sure."

"I'll tell you why," Mr Green continued. "Our Mr Oakley is Catholic, and he would not take kindly to a joke about the Papists, no matter how well put."

Mrs Haddington gasped. "No, our Mr Oakley! A Catholic officer, indeed."

Mr Green shrugged, careful to keep his voice low, giving a rather conspiratorial tone to their conversation, though Judith felt guilty to gossip and looked away as he said, "There are more and more. And why not, when we need the men? The oath we all take before we serve has something about not much caring for the Pope, of course, but men take all sorts of oaths every day."

Mrs Peggy Haddington's eyes narrowed. "I know you'll not be telling me that men do not respect the oaths they have taken. That would be something to say about my husband, indeed!"

Mr Green held up his hands. "No slight, Mrs Haddington, I assure you. Your husband is the most excellent of men and a very good friend to his fellow officers."

They looked at Mr Percival Haddington, who went to speak to Mr Haskett as Miriam carefully hid their charade. Judith smiled, reflecting that her sister was still so very young. Cheating was always a part of the games they played with their little brothers by the fireside. Perhaps she had not been in company enough to realize that implying one's host might cheat as brazenly as a young child would be impolite.

The hostess clapped her hands. "I have given you all a great deal of time, I believe! My dear Peggy, what have you for us?"

"Nothing, I'm afraid," the younger Mrs Haddington said. "We have failed to produce, again."

Judith could not account for the bitterness in Peggy's tone, but she saw Louisa-Margaretta look away, and the elder Mrs Haddington bustled over to put a hand on her daughter-in-law's shoulder.

"Now, my dear," she said, "you and your presence are quite blessing enough. We do not need anything additional." She moved swiftly to the next group. "My dear Miss Miriam St

Clair, you seem to be the writer. Will you also read to us? Were you the one who wrote most of the charade?"

The older Mr Haddington, Louisa-Margaretta's taciturn father, nodded with some enthusiasm. "We did very little, my dear. Miss Miriam St Clair thought it up."

"I can well believe it." Mrs Haddington gave a broad, affectionate smile. She plainly realized her husband was rubbish at writing poetry, and yet, she clearly loved him for the flaw just as much as she loved him for any of his virtues.

Miriam cleared her throat, going a little red as she was forced to read with the whole room's attention on her. It struck Judith that Miriam still looked very young and that, though she had been officially "out" since Christmas, the room's inhabitants were unlikely to believe it from her manner. Judith herself should have paid more attention to Miriam at the gatherings, but they had been at odds for some time. Judith could not bear to help her sister if she was to be met constantly with bitterness and anger.

She soon found herself laughing at the charade, as it was indeed full of Miriam's voice.

"My first is lovely, like a doe. My second, bright and glad. But with their union—tides of woe! Our hearths are cold and sad."

Many initial guesses were in error, from "dear heart" to "rosy"—"roe sea." Judith thought she should not speak the answer, but when nobody offered it, she was compelled to explain.

"Lady Day," she said to the company, to many groans. "Our parents have always been strict about it. Lady Day was a very firm beginning of spring in our house, and no hearth fires happened after Lady Day, even when it snowed that very night."

"That only happened once." Her father smiled.

"Twice!" Miriam and Judith said together.

"Surely nobody will hold us to those antiquated standards in Derbyshire," Mr Oakley said. "Why, it is so very cold here. Fires may be needed at the height of summer."

"Warm clothing may be needed in the summer," Mr Haskett said. "A fire after Lady Day is a terrific waste of wood."

"Do not be alarmed, ladies," Mr Green said. "My friend Mr Haskett will have you believe that officers are not allowed any sort of comfort. Depend upon it, that is far from the truth."

Judith wondered why his eyes lingered on Mr Oakley as he said it.

Colonel Chant shook his head. "I should certainly hope my men do not depend on a good blaze at any time of year," he said. "It cannot be guaranteed, even in winter."

"Well, we can all be thankful for the one we have today," Mr Percival Haddington said. "And, Mother, if you continue with these exceptionally welcoming fires, you can be assured of our company all spring, even if we have to make every card party into church, or whatever this gathering is." He took a rather large swig of wine, and both his wife and his mother looked uneasy.

The mother, however, recovered her spirits faster, clapping her hands before going over to her beloved children and holding their hands. Mr Haddington, despite the fact that his cheeks were rosy from wine, looked rather uncomfortable.

"What have you both for us, then?" she asked. "And you, dear Mr Oakley."

His smile was rather tight. "Oh, your children together composed this one. I could not have written something like it had I endless wit and time."

Mrs Haddington looked rather puzzled, but then Louisa-Margaretta began to read. "My first is like feet, my second has meat. Together they're sorry and sad. The first is to poison the second, I say. For who loves a feast before death?"

This one was not difficult for the company to guess, and there were some rather tentative declarations of "Last Supper" before it was confirmed that this was indeed the answer. But the poem was rather too funny for Judith's taste, and she saw that her father and Mrs Haddington were both taken aback. The younger Mr Haddington, taking more gulps of wine, went on a bit, while Louisa-Margaretta—who was as sacrilegious a friend as Judith had ever made—giggled beside him.

"We thought about speaking of how a cobbler's last stinks," he said. "Think of it, all these shoes going onto feet, then onto the last, then back onto feet? It is smelly work, that of a cobbler."

Mrs Peggy Haddington's face was tight. She stood, but instead of going to her husband, she went to get a refreshment.

"Well," the elder Mrs Haddington said. "Perhaps we should give the young people a moment to revel in their glory! Such wit, though I fear that yours rather missed the mark, my dears."

Thankfully, the conversation had grown loud enough to cover whatever response Mr Percival Haddington made, and Judith hurried to her friend.

"Your hair looks divine," she said. "Has Harriet suddenly become French?"

Louisa-Margaretta, who had been gazing at the spot Judith and Mrs Peggy Haddington had vacated, blinked. "What, Harriet? No. This was all Tattershall's work. Did I tell you about her? She's Peggy's lady's maid, but she does the most wonderful things with hair—and gowns too. Nobody could get this one to fit me, and she set it to rights within a day."

Judith examined her friend's glorious green gown, which made her hair and skin glow in the candlelight. It was, in some ways, not quite proper attire for Lent. Then again, Louisa-Margaretta would always look beautiful, so perhaps it was a waste for her to spend an entire season trying to create a disadvantage that nature had certainly not given her.

"Have you always been good at charades?" she asked. "I am ashamed we did not finish."

Mr Green was by their side and did not hesitate to insert himself into the conversation. "Ours would not have pleased our hostess. We did an honorable thing in our withdrawal."

Louisa-Margaretta smiled. "Oh, you soldiers! You are all so fond of honor."

"That in itself is witty," he said. "We are all very fond of our friend Honor, even those of us who find some of his tirades rather tedious."

As if on cue, Mr Haskett's voice rose above the rest. "The prince of Wales commands us all. As did his father, until this temporary weakness overtook him. I think we would do well to remember that."

Mr Oakley's voice rose just as loud. "His father had so much trouble even thinking of Catholic emancipation that Mr Pitt was ordered not to mention it, lest he bring on another fit of madness. Think of it! We criticize other nations for fighting while our leader cannot speak of the state of his nation without succumbing to a degree of lunacy not even his court of sycophants can hush up."

"But the prince of Wales," the younger Mr Haddington said, "quite a fellow, what? You knew him in London, Oakley, of course you did. And was he not a capital gent?"

The rest of the conversations had gone quiet. They all heard the menacing delicacy with which Mr Oakley set down his glass, the tiny note of it hitting the table's fine wood.

"I did know him," he said, "and he was quite a fellow for

the gaming houses or the theatre. Hardly the sort of man to run a nation. Say what you will about Napoleon Bonaparte—"

"No," Mr Haskett said, louder still. "We cannot allow such disrespect to our sovereign."

Mr Oakley leered at his fellow officer. "I *can* allow it, I assure you. Indeed, what sort of men are we if we cannot hear the truth?"

Colonel Chant finally stood. "What sort of men are we," he said quietly, "if we cannot honor our hostess? Mrs Haddington, ladies, let me apologize for my officers. We have not been often in company, and perhaps we are all more in need of society than I had realized."

It was as if he had awakened Mrs Haddington, who came rushing over. "Of course. Well, it is late, and of course you must be tired. Tempers are high when sleep is low, or so the children's nurse always told me."

"Yes," her son said with more than a hint of sarcasm. "Yes, charades can be ever so wearying. What say we go back together, Oakley, if Green and Haskett can tear themselves away from the conversation?"

The guests all left after that, making their apologies to the hostess, though Louisa-Margaretta drew her friend aside before she departed with her family.

"That's a party with dear Percival," she said. "I hope you liked it, because he will beg Mother for another one, but she will refuse for a time."

"Does he always drink so much wine?"

Louisa-Margaretta paused. "Yes, but he's usually rather fun when the wine is good. I'm not sure why he was so dull today. Perhaps Peggy could tell me, though she doesn't seem pleased with him herself."

"I will see you soon?"

"You may depend on it."

They did not leave immediately on the morrow, Mr St Clair having some calls to pay in the village. Judith found herself shivering as the sun took its time cutting through the Derbyshire mist and was thankful that her father's parishioners were quick to offer them tea, even when they could ill afford it. When they refused out of politeness, Judith found herself wishing they could have brought tea from the rectory. She cursed the custom that prohibited it. At length, after Judith had persuaded her father that the hour when respectable ladies received visitors would soon be past, they turned towards Wycliff Castle. He insisted on calling at the rectory first so they could collect Miriam, though Judith begged him to leave her at home.

"She wants company, dear," he said. "Your company and that of your friend Miss Haddington. She is lonely."

"Then she ought to find some other occupation," Judith said. "When I do bring her, she does not know how to behave. She embarrasses me."

"You can teach her," her father insisted, "and make sure she comes to no harm."

"I thought that fell to Aunt Leah," Judith grumbled. "I am not such an old maid that I can spend all my time tutoring my younger sister in the ways of society."

"Not all your time, dear," her father said, but he made no other answer.

Though Judith half expected him to talk about why Aunt Leah had returned to Essex and how their sick cousin needed her help much more than the healthy Derbyshire St Clairs did, he did not raise the subject again. It was one of the things that exasperated Judith about her father. In his years as rector, he had learned that argument was often fruitless, and his naturally placid temper was well suited for the role of peacemaker. It took much of the satisfaction out of opposing him.

All the Haddington ladies were home, as Mrs Peggy Haddington was staying with her husband's family rather than nearer the regiment. Judith wondered why Mr Percival Haddington himself did not stay with his parents, but she reflected that his duties to his regiment might require that he lodge with the other officers.

His friends, it appeared, did not share his disinclination to spend much of the day at Wycliff Castle. Mr Green was already amongst the ladies, entertaining them with tales of the younger soldiers, and Judith noticed both Miriam's countenance and her own heart brightening at the sight of the amiable young man.

Though she scolded herself, she changed her mind in the next moment. *Why should I be insensible to such agreeable company?* After all, she had convinced her father to accompany her to help show that they were in no way offended by the previous evening, Mr Percival Haddington's drunken declarations notwithstanding. It was important that they make the Haddingtons feel that the party had come off. Perhaps Mr Green was present with the same intent, and if he was, that could only be good for her friend's family.

As usual, they were not direct about the purpose of their visit, but they were soon drawn into a theological discussion. The elder Mrs Haddington rarely seemed to care about anything else.

"There is power in prayer," she said, "and I know that when we lift our voices to the Lord, we feel not only the repentance of this season but also its power."

Mr St Clair, who was not in the practice of urging people to pray aloud, only nodded. "Yes, there is power in prayer to be sure."

"And how often have I felt," Mrs Haddington continued, "that this practice of confessing our sins to our Lord, in our hearts, is vastly insufficient? We should speak of our transgressions without shame, and we should beg forgiveness not only from God but from those we have wronged."

Mr St Clair cleared his throat. "To be sure, that has been a common practice across the ages. I once heard..."

Louisa-Margaretta drew Judith over the window, where she pretended to point out something on the lawn.

"Mama will continue all morning," she murmured. "I wanted a conversation with you, but if she keeps talking about confessing sins aloud and shouting her prayers to the whole room, neither of us will be able to speak."

"We need an excursion." Judith kept her voice even lower.

She was less annoyed than Louisa-Margaretta by Mrs Haddington's public declarations of spiritual fervor. At most times, Mrs Haddington's statements centered entirely around her own experience of religion, but that did not stop her from doing good works. If Judith could have avoided Mrs Haddington's company and scrutiny, she would have considered her a woman of valor, a match for every line of the description in Psalms. But women of valor could be rather trying when one had to share a drawing room with them. As it was, Judith did her best to avoid her hostess's notice, which often involved finding excuses for a tête-à-tête with her friend when Mrs Haddington's religious passion reached its zenith.

"Miriam will wish to accompany us wherever we go," she said, her voice low. "She is insufferable now. It is as if being out means forcing herself upon company so as to exhaust every eligible young man in the neighborhood."

Louisa-Margaretta shrugged. "I do not mind her presence. She may not be discreet, but we can talk of trifles."

"I come here to escape my sister, not to prattle on with drawing room talk," Judith insisted. "Suggest that we ride together, and she will not follow. Miriam hates horses too much to agree, even with the promise of a good gossip."

Louisa-Margaretta nodded. "We may have to entertain Mr Green, then."

Judith looked at the man, who sat between Miriam and her father. He appeared just as comfortable as if he had company in his personal drawing room.

She found that she did not mind the idea of his joining them at all, though Mrs Haddington and her father might insist on a chaperone. In fact, it made the prospect of a ride in the spring damp much more enticing than it otherwise might have been.

"Mama," Louisa-Margaretta said. "It is to be a fine day. Might I invite our guests to join me for a ride?"

$\maltese$ 5 $\maltese$

In the end, it was only Mrs Peggy Haddington who joined them, and she proved a more uncertain rider even than Judith. It did not help that the spring rains had left a good deal of mud, though the ground was just hard enough for a leisurely ride. Even on the better path, Louisa-Margaretta had to take pains to ensure that none of the horses or riders got themselves into trouble. It would have been a lovely pastoral scene, reflected Judith, if not for the lingering damp. When she took the trouble to look about her, she saw some buds and new green leaves on some of the trees, and she heard more birdsong than she had noticed the last time she went riding for her picnic with Louisa-Margaretta.

Mr Green had declined, but very politely, and had taken the opportunity to walk with the ladies down to the stable. Judith could not help but feel that he paid her very particular attention. He asked her more than once whether she would not be cold, and he took care to point out some of the finer features he noticed on the house, having some interest in architecture.

Judith's interest in the house's architecture had never extended beyond the point of wondering why one family with only three members settled in Derbyshire should have any need of a castle. Even if all Louisa-Margaretta's brothers and their families had joined them, Wycliff Castle would have been absurdly large. But when Mr Green talked to her of balustrades, Judith felt as if she were rising in his estimation as well as being let in on one of his private and treasured pursuits. She was sorry when finally they reached the stables.

Theirs had been a quick departure, as there were more than enough horses to go round as well as plenty of grooms to prepare them. However, that did not give the riders any great joy. Mrs Peggy Haddington, in particular, let loose with many choice words as they walked along at a slower pace than even Judith typically demanded.

"Our horses are wasted on you, I suppose, Peggy," Louisa-Margaretta said.

Peggy laughed. "Wasted on anyone who did not grow up riding a pony round the park every day, Lou. That includes most of our lot, besides you and Percy."

Judith looked on in surprise. She had noticed that the elder Mrs Haddington did not permit anyone to shorten the names of her sons and daughters, but Peggy seemed to think nothing of it.

"Being with family must be pleasant," Judith said cautiously. "My brothers always talk of going into the army, but I do not think I could bear to have them always away from home."

"How old are they, then?"

"Let's see. Seven, six, and nearly four."

Peggy snorted. "Well, then. Plenty of time to talk some sense into them. And if you won't, plenty will. I, for one."

Louisa-Margaretta slowed her horse with some difficulty to accommodate her companions. "Now, Peggy. It might not be for you, but the St Clair boys love to talk of fighting. For all we know, they might find army life absolutely perfect."

"How would you know? Spend a good deal of time with those boys, do you? Doesn't seem likely to me."

Louisa-Margaretta sniffed. "Little boys are rather trying."

"Rather tedious, you mean. But just wait until they learn to hunt. You'll like them well enough then. You can all go off together and kill as many foxes as you like."

"I'm sure they will not hunt," Judith said, horrified. "I believe Father would not allow it."

Peggy snorted. "And when they see even ladies like Lou riding to hounds? He'll not be able to stop them."

They contemplated that. The mild incline of the slope they attempted seemed enough to make Peggy grit her teeth, and Judith wondered whether they could find a still-easier path to manage. She knew of one that was quite flat near the stream, but the water was quick and high, with flooding already starting in many places. Louisa-Margaretta, as usual, could not help but charge ahead of her companions, and she alternated between nearly cantering up the hill and keeping her horse stock-still as she impatiently picked at her elegant riding habit.

"Mrs Haddington," Judith ventured. "Do you expect to continue traveling with the army?"

Peggy gave a sharp laugh. "May as well, mayn't I, when there are no children? But it's a lonely business for an officer's wife. I can easily say that much. Percy's old colonel was married, even if his wife was a stuffy old bore. Now, with nobody to fill her place, I have no company."

Judith refrained from commenting that the lady's manners indicated she was very little in society, though that was probably true. Army men had a certain reputation, and unfortunately, Percival's behavior the previous day had very nearly confirmed it. They had also seemed very much a part of one group—she recalled the looks Percival had given Mr Oakley and the way Mr Green seemed to know what Mr Haskett intended to say before the man even opened his mouth. Clearly, as a mere wife and one not as highborn as the officers, Peggy Haddington was not a part of that group.

"Perhaps we can endeavor to find some parties for you while you are here, Mrs Haddington." Judith wondered if she might kill two birds with one stone. She was supposed to see to Miriam's happiness, and if she had to chaperone her sister about the neighborhood, she might as well help the lonely woman and see more of her friend in the bargain.

"Yes," Louisa-Margaretta said. "Let's take my sister Peggy to meet all our neighbors. They talk of nothing but farms and marriage, but by all means, it shall be very amusing for her."

"Lou," Mrs Haddington warned with a look at Judith.

But Judith was used to her friend's little barbs. "We can make a more amusing party," she insisted. "Louisa-Margaretta, you can have your mother host a dinner, and we shall make sure to be good company."

"Even if it ends with more Easter charades?"

"Trust me, Lou," Peggy said. "After Percy's little display as well as the sacrilegious rhymes we heard, your mother will never think of repeating that game."

❦   *6*   ❦

Louisa-Margaretta wanted the glistening, perfectly arranged hair that she had enjoyed the other day. She had never needed much ornamentation, but she found that she was satisfying her parents' wishes despite her natural disinclination to do anything that might tarnish the memory of the love she had enjoyed in London—the love she thought would be more than enough to satisfy her for the rest of her days.

That love will be enough, she reminded herself. But her feelings for Isaac depended on images that were just as still as the paintings she and her beloved had once stood together and admired. Though the company she currently kept did not contain any gentlemen who could match her Isaac, it had the glimmer of reality. She could speak a new thought and hear it received. She could see with her own eyes the effect her beauty had on the assembled company. It held some temptation, after all, though she was determined not to succumb.

And while she sat aloof, not allowing herself to be charmed by any of the gentlemen, she did not mind having beautiful hair. That would make the whole experience much more pleasant and might aid in strengthening her resolve.

Tattershall, however, was nowhere to be found, and Peggy was not helpful on the subject of her whereabouts. Louisa-Margaretta found her sister-in-law sitting in her bedroom, gazing out the window without any apparent care for her own toilette.

"It's only a family dinner," Peggy snapped, not looking at Louisa-Margaretta. "Apart from your St Clairs, it is men I meet with nearly every day."

Louisa-Margaretta held her head higher, feeling the strange mess that Harriet had made of her hair slip out of place. "This dinner was arranged for you, Peggy." She glared until her sister-in-law met her gaze. "You claimed to want company, and unless Mama and I are to run about herding villagers, this is all the company we are likely to find of a Wednesday evening in Lent."

Peggy's face softened. "Excuse me, Lou. I know it's kindly meant. But I don't know where you would find Tattershall. I'll find her and send her to you, that is, if you don't feel pretty enough for Percy's men."

"No." A flush crept into Louisa-Margaretta's neck, but she refused to acknowledge it. "Mama and Papa want to marry me off, but I'll have none of it. Tattershall is gentler than Harriet. That's all."

Peggy nodded. "Never marry. That's what I would tell you. There's no shame in being an old maid so long as you have two shillings to rub together."

She looked so sorrowful as she said it that Louisa-Margaretta could not keep herself from comment. "And you did not have two shillings?"

"Bless me, I didn't. But I'll not trouble you with that. Your parents have been kind to me. And your mother's asking for you. She'll be wanting you to go down."

Louisa-Margaretta went into the dining room, where she knew her mother would be supervising the particulars of the meal, only to be steered away.

"I put Mr Green in the music room, dear," she said. "He was rather early, but then, these officers are all trained in punctuality, aren't they? I thought you and dear Judith might like to play together. She is such a fine musician, and we have plenty of Bach for her."

Louisa-Margaretta sighed. "I hardly think she will play with me, Mama. I've been trying to convince her for weeks."

"Well, you're not much of a Haddington if you abandon your efforts." Her mother shepherded her into the music room. "I'll return in just a moment."

Mr Green had made himself quite at home on one of the finest chairs, though he sprang to his feet when Louisa-Margaretta entered. "Miss Haddington, a pleasure."

Propriety would have dictated that they not be left alone, but Louisa-Margaretta knew her mother could not resist overseeing every detail of the meal until it arrived on the table. Perhaps Louisa-Margaretta had done such a good job of convincing her parents that she would never marry that they felt certain she would not risk any part of her virtue. And she would not, particularly not for a creature such as Mr Green. But when he lingered over her hand after he kissed it, she was conscious of her gratitude for the empty room. The door was open, and yet, she was certain they would not be disturbed.

"I am delighted that I shall hear you play at last, Miss Haddington," he said. "And you write your own words, as well, I believe your brother said?"

She could hardly imagine that Percival spent much time speaking of the trifling amusements of his younger sister, but she nodded. "I do."

Mr Green still stood just a bit closer than ought to have been allowed. "I hope you will play and sing."

His smile was so becoming that Louisa-Margaretta stepped away. "My cousin wanted me to do both. He thought that Miss Judith St Clair and I might sell our music that way."

Mr Green smiled broadly, and Louisa-Margaretta snapped at him.

"You think it an unworthy endeavor?"

"No, only I think it is wonderful that your cousin should have recognized such talent in you. He must know you to be an enterprising young lady."

She narrowed her eyes, trying to force Mr Green's elegant clothing from her notice. Truly, had he been a plain man, he would have made a much easier conversation partner. As it was, she could not tell whether she ought to be amused or offended. "What do you know of talent? As you said yourself only a moment ago, you have never heard me play."

"Might I have the pleasure now?"

She decided that obliging him would be easier than arguing with him. Still trying not to meet his eyes but glancing at him every minute or so, she sat before her harp.

❦   7   ❦

Louisa-Margaretta had not seen the table arrangement before the company gathered, and what greeted her when she walked in was a horror.

"Welcome," her mother said as her guests settled. "I am thankful that you all could join us today. I had a meal planned in honor of Lent, and I thought, what would be more fitting than to offer a modest first course? The next course will be less so, and I even allowed some cheese to make its way into our meal later on. But I thought that this course would be perfect for this season of grace and mercy."

Louisa-Margaretta did not often blush, but she looked at their guests in horror. In front of each place sat a simple soup bowl full of clear liquid along with a slice of bread. The setting looked fit for a small child in the nursery. She was sure that when she tasted it, the "soup" would only be water. If she could be thankful for anything, let it be the fact that all the assembled company were acquainted with her mother's religious nature and would not take offense at the meagre offering that was to begin their meal.

"Thank you for thinking of the season," the rector said,

the first guest to overcome his surprise and compliment the hostess. He showed his good breeding as well as his lack of discomfort with modest offerings.

It must, Louisa-Margaretta reflected, be something he often saw in his rounds. To hear Judith tell it, they frequented the homes of very poor parishioners, and Louisa-Margaretta felt thankful that at least she did not have to go on such errands. Her mother demanded much by way of religious observance, but she was more than willing to do her pious charity rounds alone. Surely it must be torture for Judith, though she never complained.

After a prayer, which lasted an age, they were finally permitted to touch their bread and water. Louisa-Margaretta, seated next to Mr Green on one side and Peggy on the other, found that both guests were far too polite to make light of the situation.

"My mother will drive away all our guests, at least until Easter, if this is what she serves," Louisa-Margaretta grumbled, but Peggy kept her eyes on her plate. Louisa-Margaretta tried again. Surely her guests must be out of their wits to eat such fare. "Mama does not understand how to show affection to guests through the medium of food. I have told her that rich foods, pleasantly arranged, are naturally enticing to visitors. And yet, she seems to think that because she gets greater joy from a prayer, everyone else must be exactly like her."

Mr Green shook his head. "Your mother is very kind." He took a bite of bread.

The conversation around Louisa-Margaretta was so dull and stilted that she soon began listening to the rest of the table.

As usual, her mother did not cease to call attention to herself, that time by questioning the practice of hanging soldiers who had been in duels. "Surely, they ought not to hang men for dueling," Mrs Haddington said. "Is it not for God to mete out such justice, rather than men?"

Colonel Chant gave her a rather long look. Louisa-Margaretta noticed that he had not touched either his bread or his water.

"Meaning no disrespect, Mrs Haddington," he said, "but I'm not sure I would presume that the good Lord has the time or inclination to take on matters of crime and punishment in the military."

"Not all crime," she said, not to be deterred. "But hanging men for such offenses, I am convinced, is barbaric. Who are we to decide that their lives are to be cut short, any of us? Don't you agree, Mr St Clair?"

"We have all decided it," the clergyman said. "As members of this society, we have decided on the war, and that is just the same."

"Well, we have not all decided equally," Judith said, calmly but not as quietly as she usually was in company. "Those of us who cannot vote or sit in parliament have had rather less of a say."

Mrs Haddington shook her head. "Still, though, is it not a different matter when it comes to hanging a man for a duel? I simply cannot understand it."

Mr Haskett, putting his empty plate aside, took up the argument from his superior. "But you would support hanging a man for treason, would you not? Is dueling not just as serious an offense?"

She shuddered. "Treason. Well, to be honest with you, my dear, I can hardly imagine such a thing."

Percival, pushing aside his wineglass, joined the conversation for the first time. "It's not what you might expect, Mother."

Louisa-Margaretta saw how the hostess's face brightened at

his contribution. Poor Mama, she was so used to being the most sensible person in the room, the person speaking over all others and hoping her children might contribute some idea or bon mot. Louisa-Margaretta saw immediately that her brother's contribution wouldn't be a cheery one, though her mother did not.

"I'm not sure what I would expect when speaking of treason," Mrs Haddington said. "Secret assignations in public galleries? Messages woven into grain sacks?"

"It is just ordinary people," Percival said, "making poor decisions, as we sad sods are all wont to do from time to time. There is very little glamour, and though the consequences may be death, the people committing treason very seldom reflect on them."

Mrs Haddington pretended to frown. "I hope you're not speaking of the colonists, Percival. Though they were a treasonous lot, the fact that they ended up in a war meant they faced consequences indeed."

Mr Green shook his head. "I believe he's thinking of the men who want France to come to our shores, eh, Haddington? The Irish, for one. I heard they were practically issuing letters of invitation."

An exclamation rose from the company, and Miriam said, "Surely not."

Mr Green held up his hands. "I have little enough to say about them. Shall we change to a different topic? Rector, perhaps you can speak to us a bit more about Easter so we might pray before our next course."

It was, Louisa-Margaretta reflected, a rather polite way of saying that they were all starving. Indeed, she found herself wondering whether the argument would have become as heated if they might have had an ordinary meal. The wine was flowing, and though she drank little herself, she was not so naive to its effects that she could discount what many glasses of the libation might do to just as many near-empty stomachs.

Mrs Haddington, excited by the suggestion, forced Mr St Clair to lead them in another prayer.

"Dear God," he said, "we thank thee for the food before us and for the lively minds brought together at this table. We thank thee for the abundance of springtime and for those who take good care of the rich land that surrounds us."

$\approx$ 8 $\approx$

Judith was freezing after the first dinner course. Even the fires, lit though they were to honor the fact that Lady Day had not yet passed, were not enough to warm her. She hoped one of the other courses would be a hot stew. She realized that in her grief, her tendency to not eat would soon be her undoing. She had lived in a state of near-perpetual fasting, both after her mother's death and after Mr Ramsbury's departure. She had always scorned her aunt Leah's admonitions that she must eat to keep up her strength, but she suddenly felt the very practical consequences. She had left herself without any defenses against the chill, and she could hardly ask to put on her cloak at the table.

"Mama," Louisa-Margaretta said rather too loudly, indifferent to political conversation. "Can we not have the next course?"

But Mrs Haddington had been in hushed conference with her housekeeper and stood swiftly. "I am afraid I shall have to call for volunteers of my own. Dear young men, would one or two of you care to accompany me outside? I am told that the roads might already be flooded. I hope it is not so."

Mr Haskett stood at once, and Mr Oakley followed. The elder Mr Haddington did as well, though Mr Percival Haddington made no attempt to follow.

Mr Green continued speaking to Judith, though his tone held some amusement. "What a very good joke if we were all to be trapped here! It is just the sort of country house for it."

"I hope not." Judith blushed without knowing why. "My three brothers are all at home."

"Surely the servants will care for them?"

"Yes," she said, but she did not know how to explain the first pang of care she had felt for her brothers in a sennight.

There hadn't been a night in their lives when they were without a parent, and usually, the family was all together. Since their mother had died, Judith had been even more conscious of the nights when she and Miriam were away late with her father, rare though they were. Aaron, in particular, did not like to sleep until they had returned, though he never admitted it.

She looked out the window, but all was darkness. "It is only down the lane," she murmured. "But this house is on a hill, and so is the rectory, and I have heard that the road between floods at times."

"You have not seen it yourself? Must be rare, then," Mr Green said.

"We were not here last year. Mr and Mrs Haddington hired my father when the previous rector left, so we came before Christmas."

Mr Green smiled. "So, you truly can sympathize with our poor little regiment! Derbyshire seems quite wild to us."

She thought he might have laid some emphasis on the word wild, perhaps more than it deserved. And then she wondered if she was imagining it. After all, the scene was hardly one of gothic terror. At worst, she might have to stay in her friend's home, where she had already been an overnight guest on many occasions.

Those nights had been uniformly happy. She had been far from Mr Morgan Ramsbury in practical terms, as the castle was large and her hostess thought it best that she stay in a room close to Louisa-Margaretta's. But though she never ventured to open her door before she was fully dressed and absolutely awake, knowing that she was sleeping under the same roof as her beloved had brought a strange and unfamiliar thrill.

The sort that she could not allow herself to feel at the knowledge that she, in some sense, shared a very large home with Mr Green. She put down her spoon. There was, it seemed, little hope of a hearty stew.

"Perhaps we should join the others," she said. "I know the lane as well as anyone, and I should be able to tell whether my family and I can return home."

They walked towards the front door, but by then, Mrs Haddington was already coming back inside.

Despite her warm cloak, she seemed to have been soaked through during the few minutes that she must have spent surveying the land in the night. "We cannot see a great deal. But it is enough to convince us that it is not safe, especially for those who would return to the village. I am afraid we shall have to do better in the morning. Harris tells me it may be a matter of boats, though I certainly hope it shall not come to that."

"We soldiers know how to cross water in such conditions, ma'am," Mr Green said.

"Speaking of soldiers," Judith said, "Mrs Haddington, where are the men who accompanied you?"

"Oh, our Mr Oakley and Mr Haskett? They insisted upon going down a bit more, though I told them it was foolish. I'm sure they shall be in shortly."

Judith peered through the door. She could see nothing in the rain, though she thought she heard raised voices.

Soon a hand on her elbow steered her away. "Please do not concern yourself with them, Miss St Clair." Mr Green's voice and hand were both warm. "Dear Miss St Clair!" he exclaimed, blinking at her. "But you are quite cold."

Mrs Haddington started, taking hold of Judith at once. "My dear, are you well? It must be the rain. It chills one to the bone. I thank God you did not come out with us. You must go to bed at once! I shall see that you are in the room next to your usual one. We have had to change our arrangements a bit to accommodate all our dear visitors. You poor, sweet girl, why did you not tell us you were ill?"

And so it followed that Judith, who was troubled by nothing more than her lack of food, was sent to bed without dinner. Even the modest courses of vegetables that she had imagined—with perhaps a morsel of fish—would have warmed her. Instead, she huddled under the covers, trying to convince herself to sleep with a very empty stomach. Her family had always been blessed with food, even in years of poor harvests, and the sensation was an unfamiliar one.

When at last she felt as if she could bear it no longer, she took the dressing gown that her hosts had provided—it looked too unfashionable to have ever been Louisa-Margaretta's—and stepped into the hall. The gown was meant for a much taller woman, probably Mrs Haddington herself, and it dragged on the floor.

The house should have been quiet, but the sound of the rain and wind made the place seem alive. She saw a candle down the hall and ducked back into her room, closing the door but watching through the keyhole.

It was enough. Mrs Peggy Haddington was the one about, which seemed strange to Judith at first. Then she reflected that Peggy's room was next to the one Judith had been given and next to Louisa-Margaretta's, so if she wished to visit her husband, she might well wish to quit it. It was also rather strange that Mr Percival Haddington's room did not adjoin that of his wife's. Judith knew that very-well-to-do families might have separate bedrooms for husbands and wives, but she thought that a connecting door was a tacit acknowledgment of the marriage vows.

Cheeks burning, Judith withdrew her face from the keyhole. She felt just as ashamed as if she had seen an even more private scene and resolved not to stir outside her bedroom, not even for a bit of food.

She heard footsteps, though, on the stairs, at least two sets. And they sounded heavy, like they belonged to gentlemen. She thought she caught some of what they said.

"Get out in the morning..."

It was certainly a man's voice. She could not make out which officer it was or if it might be Mr Haddington.

"Now, my friends, my brothers."

That would likely be Mr Percival Haddington, then. He had all his friends about, and he certainly had a great deal of brothers. Louisa-Margaretta used the same tone of annoyance when talking about every brother except Percival, but Judith suspected they were kind enough fellows in truth.

Still hungry and uneasy but shivering again from her time outside the blankets, she huddled in the bed without removing the dressing gown and made another attempt at sleep.

＊ *9* ＊

The morning dawned clear. Louisa-Margaretta was glad of it, for she wished that all the guests would go and did not intend to share her castle for much longer.

She was not ashamed to admit that she wished her sister-in-law Peggy gone. In all her previous visits, Peggy had been a source of fun and gaiety, a happy contrast to her more serious sisters-in-law and a bit like the sister Louisa-Margaretta had longed for all her life. But on her current visit, Peggy could not be distracted from her melancholy, and Louisa-Margaretta's needs seemed to quite escape her. Indeed, only days before, Peggy had promised to find Tattershall then had apparently forgotten, and all evening, Louisa-Margaretta had suffered with the droopy mound of hair that Harriet had somehow fastened directly to her skull. Even after dinner, Peggy hadn't bothered to apologize but had gone off to the kitchens without speaking to Louisa-Margaretta.

Louisa-Margaretta had even observed her sister-in-law sitting near the entrance to the wing of the house they didn't yet use. What would have been the servants' entrance was practically deserted, and the staircases remained empty and dusty. But Peggy often sat outside, as long as it was not raining, looking over the hills as if they would give her some answer to her troubles. As far as Louisa-Margaretta could tell, the melancholy woman never found her answer. Louisa-Margaretta had thought once of going out to speak to Peggy but had decided against it. Though she would not admit it, she was annoyed that Peggy did not consider herself fortunate. Percival, for all his fondness for wine, was not a dullard like some husbands, and Louisa-Margaretta did not understand why her sister squandered the relative freedom that a married woman was granted in society.

Judith had nothing but pity for Peggy, but Louisa-Margaretta thought Judith was more deserving of it. She carried out the duties her mother would have had in the parish, not to mention caring for her brothers and sister, all with a broken heart. Peggy, as an army wife, might have had a very gay time of it. Instead, she complained incessantly, longed for children, longed to live in one place for more than a season, and made every meal rather tedious with her gloom.

Louisa-Margaretta realized with some real pleasure that breakfast was not likely to be as tedious as their other meals, as Peggy rarely came down, preferring Tattershall to bring her a tray in bed. And after the fasting meal of the previous day, in which only very modest and bland dishes of potatoes and soup had followed the bread and water, Louisa-Margaretta was hungry. She realized with a prickle that she also looked forward to the officers' company over breakfast, particularly the energetic Mr Oakley and the rather sympathetic Mr Green. Though Mr Haskett did not seem to have any sense of fun, his features were pleasing, and any of them would make for a livelier breakfast table than Louisa-Margaretta's father.

But before she could make up for the unpleasant and

modest dinner, she encountered her mother, fully dressed for a walk and wearing a frown that looked as out of place on her normally joyful face as it might have looked on the Queen's.

"Darling, have you seen Mr Oakley? He's not in his bed, and I can't imagine him leaving in such weather." She paused a moment to speak to Tattershall, confirmed that Peggy was yet asleep, then turned back to Louisa-Margaretta.

Louisa-Margaretta yawned. "It's hardly a decent hour. Who noticed him missing? He must be walking."

"In all this mud? Certainly not. And if he has gone, he won't have gone far. The roads are still flooded."

"What does Colonel Chant say?"

"I intend to wake him. But you have not seen Mr Oakley anywhere?"

Louisa-Margaretta nearly laughed at the worry on her mother's face. It was as if it had suddenly occurred to her that she was housing both unmarried young ladies and spirited soldiers under her roof. "No, Mama, I haven't seen anyone. Not even Judith, and she is usually up early."

"Well," Mrs Haddington said, "I will organize the men, and they shall all go out and search. I am sure one of them can find him. Percival was always quite good at hunting."

Mrs Haddington had not done it intentionally, but she'd needled her daughter. They used to have an old master who had thought the world of Louisa-Margaretta's brothers, and after hunts, he would spend a great deal of time with Mrs Haddington, praising her sons. He had hated that Louisa-Margaretta came at all and wouldn't have allowed it had her father not made it clear that no hunts were ever to take place without his youngest child.

Louisa-Margaretta, in fact, had been the best hunter of all her brothers, and Percival the worst. Riding bored him, and he never learned to follow the dogs. As like as not, he would ride part of the hunt, turn around, and raid the kitchens for tarts or sneak wine with one of his friends. But Mrs Hadding-ton, who never rode herself if she could help it, had no way of knowing that her daughter's performance rivaled that of any experienced hunter.

Louisa-Margaretta knew how to find Mr Oakley and did not wish to go alone, though she knew that no woman was likely to help her. It was time to call on a friend.

Judith was uncommonly difficult to rouse. "I got almost no sleep," she moaned. "And I'm starving."

"We all are," Louisa-Margaretta snapped. "We starved last night, and we are starving still. But you must come with me! I know the grounds better than any of those men, and on horseback, we shall be the first to find Mr Oakley. Perhaps he has gone for an assignation in a little cottage. I did hear some sort of rumor. Or was it something I got from Harriet?"

"Didn't you get to eat the other courses?" Judith rubbed her eyes.

"Yes, and they were easily as ghastly as the first, only the whole thing was twice as dull without you there." Louisa-Margaretta fought to pull the blankets off her friend.

"I'm supposed to be ill," Judith said.

"Are you?"

"No, but I would like to eat."

"Goodness, stop being such an old woman! I'll find you something from the kitchens on our way, shall I?"

Judith sprang out of bed. "Oh, please do. And your warmest cloak. I'm already frozen. I'm sure mine will not be enough."

❦   10   ❦

If Heaven hears the prayers I continually make for you, your days will be prolonged, and you will bury me. — *Heloise to Abelard, Letter IV*

J udith noted with some surprise that she and Louisa-Margaretta were the only people looking for horses. They passed Mr Haskett and Mr Percival Haddington on the stairs, both wearing their uniforms and looking drawn, but it seemed the soldiers had some plan of searching the grounds that did not involve riding.

Though she still felt cold, and awkward on the horse, the bread and cheese that her friend had demanded kept her upright. And the warm cloak did help. She had never felt truly ill and wished that Mrs Haddington had understood that she was only hungry. If she had stayed with the company for the rest of dinner, at least she might have enjoyed some discourse with Mr Green or Mr Oakley or another agreeable guest.

The trouble was that there were no other agreeable guests. Colonel Chant seldom spoke. Mr Haskett talked only of the army, and Mr Percival Haddington showed no interest in anyone who was not a brother officer. The elder Haddingtons were the same as always. Louisa-Margaretta's father always tried to speak with Judith but seemed mostly deprived in terms of his powers of conversation, and Mrs Haddington talked far too much. Judith always felt guilty around Mrs Haddington because, though they shared the same faith nominally, the modes in which they expressed it were so very different that Christianity seemed positively dangerous as a subject of conversation. Judith never would have felt at ease leading a group of people in prayer, though she said her prayers faithfully each morning and evening. The Bible itself spoke to her, but many conventions of religious life did not, including Easter. She had felt for some time that it was ghastly to celebrate an act of brutality, resurrection or not, and the connection between "devout" passion plays and contemporary acts of cruelty against innocent Jewish families was not lost on her. Judith was thankful that the dramatic spectacles had gone out of fashion many years before, though her father always mentioned them when he complained that Easter celebrations were becoming too theatrical. Judith hoped that Mrs Haddington would feel similarly if pressed, but it was hard to say. At times, Judith struggled to separate religious devotion from blind zealotry, and she never knew just how many of her friend's mother's mad impulses she would be obligated to indulge.

Lost in thought, she had allowed her horse to walk slower and slower, and Louisa-Margaretta had trotted ahead. The mist of the morning still had not fully cleared, though the day promised to be fair once it did.

"Judith!" Louisa-Margaretta called. "Come this way. If we see nothing here, must he not be in the woods?"

"We'll get stuck in the mud," she said, but her friend made no answer. And Judith noticed with some surprise that her friend seemed to lead them on a fairly safe path from mud.

Though the castle's three low sides were flooded, the rockier slope behind had been spared. It was there that they came to the clearing in the woods where they found Mr Oakley's body. Louisa-Margaretta stopped short, all her bravado lost. She could scarcely speak. Judith also lost her breath, but she found it more quickly. Ministering to the dead and dying had always been part of her father's duties, and though she had not expected Mr Oakley's death, the sight of a body was not quite as shocking to her as it was to Louisa-Margaretta.

After she struggled off her horse, she walked over and her breath eased out of her in a deep sigh. There was no mistaking the sight. Mr Oakley may not have died long ago, but he was certainly not alive. He had been shot, and a gun lay next to him. No blood stained his fine red uniform jacket, though she noticed a great deal of it on the shirt he wore beneath. The jacket had not been buttoned properly. This surprised her at first, but she and Mr Green had had a conversation about the uniform only the previous evening.

"The buttons aren't practical," Mr Green had complained. "If I ever need to enter a battle after dressing myself in a hurry, I shall simply be late."

Judith had only smiled. "You're hardly likely to have a man to help you at the front, I believe."

He had said something very like, "Yes, but I might hope to have a woman," but in such a low voice that she could not quite be sure.

Poor Mr Oakley was unlikely to need help with his buttons ever again. Judith spent a moment praying over him then turned to her friend. "You go for help," she said quietly. "I'll stay here."

"But you might be in danger," Louisa-Margaretta said, and

Judith could almost hear her friend's rapid heartbeat. "If the murderer should return?"

Judith sighed. "This was not an ordinary murder."

Louisa-Margaretta made as if to grab Judith's arm, her voice louder. It was plain that she did not want to get closer to the corpse. "No, it was not! There is a gun! All the more reason I should worry. Surely you do not think that Mr Oakley walked all this way only to shoot himself."

Judith shook her head. "Of course not. He came to a flat, isolated place, wearing his uniform, and carrying a gun."

"Then, what are you saying? And why should we not both fear for our lives?"

"Louisa-Margaretta," Judith said patiently. "We spoke of this only recently, remember?"

"Spoke of what?"

"Look at him. It is plain to see that Mr Oakley died in a duel."

11

After Louisa-Margaretta finally left, Judith did not have to wait long for the army to arrive.

They came all at once, Mr Haskett, Mr Percival Haddington, and Mr Green, all under the command of Colonel Chant, and they did not let her stay for a moment. Their bearing seemed different, both straighter and more mournful. It was as if they had only become soldiers because of the unfortunate event.

"I can ask my father to come pray over him," Judith said quietly.

"No," Mr Haskett said sharply. "This is an army matter now."

Louisa-Margaretta pulled at Judith's arm, eager to be out of sight of the corpse. "Come, Judith. I will help you."

And so she rode off with her friend, who had been shaking. Between Judith's poor seat and Louisa-Margaretta's shock, they did not come quickly back to the stables. Judith was eager to speak but received few responses from her friend.

"It seems strange to fight a duel here," she said. "Not only unseemly, as they were guests, but also very strange, considering the legality."

"Our sort is always dueling," Louisa-Margaretta said sharply.

"And getting away with dueling," Judith said, her reply rather crisp. "It remains illegal, however, especially for those without a great deal of money."

Louisa-Margaretta made no reply.

"The timing was very odd," Judith said. "Who could have the energy to fight a duel after a simple supper of bread and water?"

At last, she got half a smile out of her friend. "There was more after you left, I told you. Not a great deal, though."

"They quarreled," Judith said, "Mr Oakley and the other officers, but it all felt very ordinary. Who would fight a duel over words like that? It seems they always would have disagreed about the prince of Wales, but I hardly see how that justifies a duel."

Louisa-Margaretta shook her head. "Surely you don't think it was one of the officers who shot Mr Oakley."

Judith frowned. "I'm afraid that is the only explanation that makes sense. Who else would fight a duel with him? Who else here would even have such a gun?"

But before Louisa-Margaretta could answer, they stopped speaking, noting that they were no longer unobserved.

12

The older Mrs Haddington, rushing out to meet them, went to Judith first. "My dear Judith, how terrible for you!"

Louisa-Margaretta, who dismounted from her horse, glared at her mother.

Judith, cowed by her friend's reaction, attempted to turn the hostess's attention to the young lady who most needed her help. "It was Louisa-Margaretta who found him," she mumbled. "I would have had no idea where to go."

"Yes, but you stayed with him, my poor dear," Mrs Haddington said. "I don't know why they did not take your father! I shall find him and get a horse for him so he may go say a prayer."

"Judith already said she would tell him," Louisa-Margaretta snapped. "Colonel Chant doesn't want anyone to come near. He's not happy that there was dueling in his regiment."

Mrs Haddington gasped. "Why, surely, there was not!"

Judith looked at her friend, unsure how to answer. She did not want to describe the scene she had witnessed or her certainty that the spot had been chosen because it suited both participants. It had taken them some minutes to get there on horseback and must have been quite a trek on foot. She could hardly think that Mr Oakley would have gone to the trouble had he wished to kill himself, and besides, he certainly could not have gotten his jacket back on.

Louisa-Margaretta's tone was still clipped. Judith shook off the mother and took her friend's arm, but Louisa-Margaretta turned away.

"I'm afraid Judith saw it first, and I agree. Nobody but one of the regiment men would want to duel with Mr Oakley, so Colonel Chant wishes to find the culprit."

"But only imagine," Mrs Haddington said. "I spoke to all the young men this morning. They were out of sorts, perhaps, as one might be after spending the night away from one's bed. But not one of them killed their friend. I am quite certain."

Louisa-Margaretta spoke the question on Judith's mind. "How? How can you possibly know?"

Judith wondered if Louisa-Margaretta had also thought back to the previous murder that had puzzled the household, though initially, everyone had said it was a suicide. At that time, Mrs Haddington had not wanted to believe a murder had even taken place, so surely her assurance that neither her dear Percival nor Mr Green nor Mr Haskett had shot anyone was rather suspect.

"I have raised many young men," she said, "and in this case, I can safely promise that not one of them knows what happened."

Judith did not dare to exchange a look with her friend. "Well, I had better go and find my papa. It is possible that they will call for him, after all, and he must be told." She walked back into the house.

13

Louisa-Margaretta took the steps quickly, fuming. She saw that it had taken some time to call off the search.

Harriet apologized for the dust she brought into Louisa-Margaretta's room. "They had us searching the attics, miss, and they are so large. Only there wasn't anybody there—"

"Do not make yourself uneasy," Louisa-Margaretta snapped, which only made Harriet jump and look much more uneasy than she had. "Go and find Tattershall, then. She will help me."

Tattershall came in with an absence of both nerves and dust, and Louisa-Margaretta found her brisk efficiency soothing. If anything, Tattershall smelled of soap, and the uniform she wore looked freshly pressed. She did not complain about the mud on Louisa-Margaretta's clothing, as Harriet surely would have, and by the time Louisa-Margaretta herself was attired in one of her best day dresses, she felt a bit less fluttery.

Her heart quickened again, though, when she saw Judith arguing with her little sister, Miriam.

"You have no reason to stay here," Judith said. "You will only be in the way, and our brothers have been waiting for one of us to return."

"It may as well be you or Papa." Miriam's lower lip trembled. "The boys would want one of you more. I can help here."

"What do you think you can possibly accomplish?"

Louisa-Margaretta, stepping between them, gave silent thanks that she had no sisters. Miriam seemed to grow more petulant and troublesome by the day.

"You could both help," she said sternly, "by accompanying me down to breakfast. None of us have had anything to eat all day, and as we had precious little yesterday, I'm sure we are all in very great need of refreshment."

They walked down together, both the St Clair sisters sullen and silent at first, but Miriam became notably more animated when she saw the young Mrs Haddington in the parlor.

"Come have some breakfast, dear." Peggy looked distracted.

Louisa-Margaretta idly wondered if her sister-in-law had been in love with the late Mr Oakley. After all, Peggy had been dressing in clothes that were both finer and more flattering than usual, and Louisa-Margaretta imagined that was hardly typical of an army wife. She had initially decided that it was her mother's doing, as the elder Mrs Haddington loved to see her children and her charity cases well dressed, but Peggy had possibly finally attempted to make the most of her looks.

Louisa-Margaretta had gotten rather a shock the previous Christmas when her mother had revealed one of the secrets of marriage. Apparently, many men and women did not take it amiss if one or both parties took a lover. Adultery seemed much more scandalous than anything that happened between the husbands and wives themselves, though the latter topic was the one most likely to be spoken of when unmarried ladies were sent from the room—though often not quite adequately warned away from the keyhole. The secret of acceptable adultery was much better kept, and Louisa-Margaretta found that she still had difficulty believing it.

Apparently, according to Mrs Haddington, it was not at all uncommon—and considered widely pardonable—for married people to fall in love and have affairs, provided they went about it in the "right" fashion and did not cause trouble or embarrassment for anyone. Louisa-Margaretta thought the idea shameful and much preferred her method of remaining both crossed in love and unmarried. She saw absolutely no point to marriage itself if either party did not entirely respect the vows, and she said that if any husband of hers ever strayed for so much as an hour, he should be out on his ear.

Mrs Haddington had preached forgiveness, which was rather rich, given she was one of the most faithful adherents to the laws that God had set down for men. It was hard to accept the doctrine of forgiveness from a woman who looked askance every time a visitor so much as mentioned the idea of eating meat on a Friday. No, whatever Mrs Haddington's reason for begging Louisa-Margaretta to be forgiving, it could not have come from her past indiscretions. Louisa-Margaretta suspected that her mother was trying to help her adjust to the idea because one of her brothers had, or was having, an affair, though no gossip of that sort had reached her ears. Apparently, if it was so common a choice for rich men, it was unlikely that they all were faithful.

And that made her wonder not only about Peggy but also about Percival.

❧ 14 ❧

J udith would have pressed her father to stay on, but he was firm upon the point. He intended to say the blessing, then they would be off directly. She and her sister were not to leave the breakfast room, or at least the little parlor beside it.

Judith, who gained a great deal of energy from her breakfast, did not agree with her father but knew she could not change his mind. Though she had only just touched her food at first, wondering at the strange expression in Mrs Peggy Haddington's eyes as she spoke kindly to Miriam, Judith had soon realized how hungry she was. Apparently, any Lenten directions to the cook had been roundly ignored that morning, for the dishes were just as ample as always. As Judith regained her strength, she found herself wondering at the Haddington breakfasts. How lovely it would be to sleep each morning and take absolutely no role in the preparations yet eat richer food than they ever seemed to have at the rector. Before spending time with Louisa-Margaretta, Judith had never expected to desire wealth, but she knew she would always envy certain luxuries at Wycliff Castle.

After several minutes of staring out the window, Judith contrived to go upstairs with Louisa-Margaretta only because her ministrations had not been enough to make her dress fit for company and she had no other. It held not only mud but the unmistakable scent of wet horse. Her father said sternly that she was to return as soon as she had made herself presentable.

But her father knew nothing of fashion, and if Miriam did not give her away, Judith thought she might have time for a game of cribbage.

Louisa-Margaretta produced the board from deep within her wardrobe, along with a set of cards too worn to be missed. Mrs Haddington disapproved of cards generally, and she had always disliked the sight of her daughter playing cribbage with unmarried gentlemen. It remained to be seen whether this disapproval lingered with Louisa-Margaretta's only prospect being a young man who was not eligible in the least, but it seemed only too likely that Mrs Haddington's vehement disapproval of gambling would continue.

Judith, who generally did not gamble for want of funds, loved the game. It had never been a favourite in her household, but she found that all the shuffling and the required addition gave her plenty of time to think. She and Louisa-Margaretta had made a habit of bringing out the board whenever they needed to have a serious conversation. Louisa-Margaretta would give her entire opinion, even when nobody had asked, but her friend often required the help of a distraction such as a silly card game.

Judith won a great deal of points from her first hand and her first crib and, in the flush of victory, put forth her opinion. "It is better that we know as little of what happened to Mr Oakley as we can," she ventured. "For his dueling partner, who is certainly a man, must have had a private quarrel with him. I see no reason to suppose they will come after us."

"Not with violence, perhaps," Louisa-Margaretta said. "But with ideas of matrimony? What then?"

Judith ventured a smile. "Were you not telling me of the joys of celibacy, a life of being eternally crossed in love? Surely you do not think any of your brother's companions a good match."

Her friend seriously considered the question. "Not in terms of temperament, I suppose. Do you not think Miriam might be in some danger? She was staring at each of them in turn during our humble meal. Perhaps she likes them better than any of our nearest neighbors, and I would not fault her for that."

Judith blushed and discarded one good card and one bad, which became evident as soon as the shared card was turned.

"I hope nothing in my sister's manner gave you the impression that she would have her head turned by a solider."

Louisa-Margaretta's manner remained easy, and when Judith failed to call all her points, Louisa-Margaretta stole them with a smile.

"She would hardly be the first," she said. "And it might not be terrible for her. After all, she is out, and don't forget that my own Percival is a soldier. I should hope that neither of you has particular scorn for the profession."

Judith winced, realizing that in defending her sister, she had come close to insulting her friend's family. "Of course not. It is only that I thought her full young for such a thing. And I am used to thinking of all soldiers as serious, like your brother's friend Mr Haskett."

"Mr Honor Haskett, yes. He is serious, but Percival tells me his temper interferes with his attempts to portray himself as living up to his name. Honorable in his better moments, perhaps, but not quite such a fine example of gentlemanly behavior when he is angry."

Judith blinked. "And you fear his temper might have taken him so far as murder?"

She put down her cards, her heart fluttering at the idea of Miriam receiving attention from a violent man. It was an evil of which neither she nor her friend could be insensible, though one that she had seen more often. Her parents had been moved, more than once, to help establish women far from their violent husbands. And even those acts were rare enough, as first one had to learn a truth that so many kept hidden. Judith's mother had always maintained that a divorce ought to be easier to obtain, and while the rector had never agreed from a spiritual point of view, he was quick to point out to his daughters that the choice not to marry was always superior to such a situation.

Louisa-Margaretta only shrugged. "I have already told you, Judith, and you make me sound like a fool to repeat it. We are neither of us likely to be killed in a duel. We are just as likely to be killed on the battlefield."

"If Napoleon Bonaparte's army manages to come ashore, you mean?"

"No! I mean we are quite safe from whatever soldiers are doing, either in battle or at home. We shall not be dueling, and it is foolish to think that any of those soldiers will be eager to challenge each other now. But your sister's heart may not be safe, and I am not convinced that yours is either. Besides, with Colonel Chant running about, talking of his ideas on the matter, we will have a very dull Easter with nearly no company. We may as well find something to do."

Judith, unlike her friend, never suffered from lack of occupation in her household. Her role as her mother's replacement kept her days busy. She had noticed of late that some of the evening visits seemed to tire her father, who was no longer young, and she had resolved to do more of them herself. Perhaps she could even press Moses and Aaron into service, at least in the households with other similarly energetic young children.

"I am sure your mother will want a quiet house," she said. "My father will find me in a moment."

"Then say you will join me, Judith! We are just as likely to get to the truth of the matter as the stodgy old colonel."

Judith drew in her breath. "He is your brother's superior officer!"

"For now, yes. But if he is eavesdropping on two young ladies in a private home, he ought to be ashamed of himself."

Judith looked about, her heart racing, sending her friend into fits of laughter.

The notion created in her a fresh horror. "Oh, Louisa-Margaretta, you really should not laugh at me. Neither of us should laugh. Poor Mr Oakley, and yours is a house in mourning!"

"Oh, I know, I know. I have relatives enough that we are most often in mourning for something, and I shall be a good little spinster and find my least-becoming black dress in a moment. But your face, Judith!"

Shaking her head, Judith composed her expression then went downstairs with her friend. To her great relief, there was no sign of Colonel Chant and no very great chance that he had heard them. They could hardly have anticipated that keeping their intentions secret from the colonel would not be enough to protect them from the force of his anger.

❧ 15 ❧

The next morning brought nothing more irregular than a well of questions from the youngest St Clairs. Though their father had enjoined Judith and Miriam, using the strongest language of which he was capable, to avoid the evils of gossip, it was in vain. Gossip, unlike dueling, was a vice observed equally amongst both sexes. It was a weakness in those susceptible mortals occupying all stations of life.

"Did you hear the duel?" Aaron asked. "I heard there were pistols at dawn, and the whole neighborhood could smell the gunpowder! Even we could smell it!"

"Child." Their father raised his brows without his usual mildness. "Come have some breakfast. You'll go hungry otherwise."

"I am sure you smelled only your crumpets, dear," Judith said.

The glorification of violence was one of the few behaviors her father did not allow, even in his youngest children, and she was eager that gunpowder not be mentioned again.

"Who roasted them without me to see to it?" she asked.

Her youngest brother scowled. "I wanted to, for I was hungry. But after I burned two, Moses took them all from me."

"I didn't want them to go to waste!"

The subject of crumpets proved even more fascinating to the young boys than the topic of gunpowder. But Judith had no sooner turned to her breakfast than she was accosted by Miriam.

"What did Miss Haddington say to you?" she asked. "I'm sure she has her own ideas of what happened to Mr Oakley."

Judith was relieved. At least she could defend her own honor. "I told her that it was not for us to inquire," she said primly. "The army will look into the matter, and I do not approve of dueling."

"But, Judith," Miriam said, "which of the soldiers could have done it? I know you wish to know. I will not pretend to be the only one here who is curious."

Judith frowned, remembering what Louisa-Margaretta had warned about Miriam's head being turned by a soldier.

"Why are you curious?" she asked. "None of them is your particular friend, unless I am mistaken."

Miriam heard the solemnity of the tone and flounced away, only to return with a promise. "You like to do things for the Haddingtons. Well, now they need help understanding what has transpired in their very garden, and I want to help them."

Judith shook her head. Though she could not say why she felt the matter was dangerous, she disagreed with Louisa-Margaretta's assurances of their safety. "It was hardly in their garden," she said. "If it had been closer to the house, we could have walked instead of taking horses."

"Where was it exactly?" Miriam asked. "None of the servants seem to agree."

"Miriam," Judith said a little too loudly. With a glance at

her brothers, she lowered her voice. "Neither of us should be gossiping about this. It was most unfortunate and absolutely against the law, and that is where we will leave it."

"You want to help as much as I do," her sister persisted.

"If you are so eager to be of use," Judith said curtly, "perhaps you will accompany us this morning as we call on a very deserving family."

It was as if she had taken a whole lemon and squeezed it directly into her sister's tea. Miriam, quite plainly, could not stomach the thought. And Judith had known as much when she suggested it to her sister. If Judith found her father's visits tedious at times, she reproached herself and endeavored to think of kindness and humility. When Miriam found the visits tedious, she tried to get out of them, and she took few pains to spare the parishioners' feelings. In fact, her favourite thing to claim was a sick headache. She used the excuse so often that it tended to be viewed with either open suspicion or fond indulgence. Judith could not think it would pass muster with the family they were about to visit.

"Fine," Miriam said. "But next time you see the Haddingtons, I will accompany you."

A year ago, or even a season ago, Judith could have insisted that Miriam not take such a step. But both Miriam's bitter tone and the loud noise her chair made when she pushed it into the breakfast table before running off made such a conversation impossible.

Indeed, as Judith and her father walked out for their visit, she wished that she had tried to flatter and persuade Miriam into going. The morning was chill and foggy again, and in every shadow, she saw a murderous soldier. She started so many times near walls and hedgerows, even those that were not yet fully green, that her father offered his arm.

"Perhaps I should not have brought you," he said solicitously. "You have had a shock, my dear. You had better have stayed home with your sister."

Judith tried to laugh, though her pride was wounded. Louisa-Margaretta's similar accusation of cowardice the day before had rankled less than her father's. She had not been open about her feelings, and yet, her elderly papa called her weak.

"I am quite well, Papa," she said. "Indeed, I imagine it was more of a shock for you."

He shook his head, his expression as placid as ever. "A grief, yes, but not a shock. I have seen a great deal of death. If anything was rare, it was the colonel's reaction."

Judith, in spite of herself, could not stop from asking, "He was angry, then?"

Her father nodded. "That is not an uncommon reaction. He has lost one who, in a sense, was in his care and who passed in a manner that he must not have expected. But it was as if he believed that, by dueling, Mr Oakley somehow deserved his lot. The colonel did not even wish him to have a Christian burial, though I believe I may have convinced him."

They walked some time in silence. Judith remembered her resolution not to investigate, to leave the soldiers to themselves. And she also remembered the statements that her friend had made. Though she hardly thought it was likely one of the men would become her brother-in-law, she could not help admitting that the prospect of uncertain death at the hands of the French might make the men reckless. Indeed, she had heard of many hasty marriages in wartime. Her father had even performed one with no time for banns to be read, as the young man's ship was to leave the harbor, and by rights, he should not have done it. But his heart was moved by the plight of two young people who, fearing separation by death, wanted to be joined together in matrimony first.

Judith shook her head to free herself of the recollection.

It made her situation hardly seem romantic. The couple whom her father had married had put love above all else, whereas she and Mr Morgan Ramsbury allowed a mere difference of religion to separate themselves forever. The thought gave rise to her greatest fear—that he did not truly love her. *Who could say that he, indeed, loved me if he was not willing to come back to the church for my sake?*

Her father turned into the little lane where the Barnes family lived, and she was forced to put Mr Ramsbury out of her mind. He was so often there that she thought, like some madwoman, she would start imagining him to be actually with her many hours of the day. But she knew she would need all her energy to face the matriarch of the Barnes family, and if she let down her guard by imagining the subtleties of Mr Ramsbury's look, the warmth of his arm through her gloved hand, she would be lost.

S he was thankful, at least, that they went to a familiar home. The village was small, and the harsh surrounding mountains seemed sufficient to keep most would-be inhabitants away. Indeed, for their first months in Derbyshire, Judith herself had thought the place wild and unpleasant. Even then, she knew she would be better suited to a milder climate. She could bear the cold because she had been raised not to complain, but in her heart, she disliked the bitter chill in spring, one that she knew might well last into June. Her aunt Leah had made rhapsodic comments about the beauty that summer would bring, but Leah had never spent a single summer's day far from Essex, so Judith was not certain her aunt knew anything about the subject.

Louisa-Margaretta was better suited to the wild hills, with their unceasing snow, rain, and floods. She was an explorer, always out on her horse or ready to plan a grand journey. Judith, on the other hand, had been thankful for the flooding only because it excused her father from some of his duties. Despite the great commotion in the hall, it was too muddy for them to call on anyone but their nearest neighbors. Even then, Judith thought, another rector would have stayed indoors. But her father was very fond of the Barnes family and thought they would need cheer. Mrs Prudence Barnes was always busy with the little ones, and she had her own mother to care for as well.

Of course, the elderly do not always wish to receive the attentions of their children and grandchildren. Old Mrs Maxwell looked little inclined to welcome cheer or dispense it herself. She met them at the door with a glare as they tried to get the worst of the mud from their boots before entering.

"A sorry business," she said. "There's trouble at that hall. Trouble with this family."

Her daughter, Mrs Barnes, took her arm. "Mama, there's a terrible draught. Oh, Mr St Clair, you are very welcome, and Miss St Clair. You need not have come to see us. I am sure the roads are not safe."

"Muddy but quite safe." Judith smiled politely, taking the chair that was offered.

As usual, the older Barnes children snapped at the younger ones to quiet down, and the admonishments did not work for more than a moment. Judith thought of how her mother would have loved it. Though her father was fond of children, he did not usually join in their games and was just as happy to sit and drone on about Leviticus while the children provided a tableau of family chaos. But Judith's mama loved children's games, and she would run to the children, insist upon joining, and have them all in fits of laughter.

Miriam would do the same, Judith thought, if she were only patient enough to take an interest in some of their father's visits.

"We hope the roads will dry soon." Mrs Barnes smoothed her skirts then got up to see about a bit of cake for her visitors. "I'm afraid the children may have eaten all our cake. But I'm sure we have something."

"Please, don't trouble yourself," Judith and her father said in unison, and she tried not to smile. She had heard him utter the same phrase to so many parishioners over the years that it fell off her tongue before she realized she was speaking.

Mrs Maxwell found interest in only one topic. "Before those Haddingtons came, I am sure we never used to have such goings-on. The work of the devil—first that sad business at Christmas and now dueling. We are not that sort of village, Mr St Clair. We were once respectable."

Judith looked carefully at her father, wondering if he would perceive some personal slight as the parish's spiritual caretaker, but he was all concern for the elderly woman.

"It is tragic indeed," he said, "and alarming to all the ladies, I cannot wonder."

Mrs Maxwell scoffed. "Alarming to the men, I should have thought. They are the ones who would duel, and those soldiers have no scruples. They are rather worse and rather better at a card table than they ought to be. I am sure you can understand my meaning. It shouldn't be anyone's living, playing at cards."

Mrs Barnes came back in, and the apple tart that she apologized for was sweet and tender. Judith realized that, once again, she had not been eating as she ought, a fact that Mrs Maxwell usually pointed out when she was not occupied in the sad dealings of the soldiers.

"I am sure the soldiers make their living out of their pay, Mama," Mrs Barnes said after gently scolding one of her youngest daughters to come away from the fire, then resorting to picking the child up and holding out pieces of tart to the little one's plump hands.

"Not the officers," Judith said. "At least, not early on.

They are expected to have other income and to be gentlemen. And I suppose most of them are."

Mrs Maxwell shook her head. "They take all kinds now.
Scoundrels, you mark my words. That Corsican may be a
devil, but that doesn't mean we shouldn't have quality officers
ourselves. Evil met with evil, I should say. Dueling soldiers!"

Mrs Barnes, perhaps, ought to have known that her
mother could not easily be turned from a subject, but her fear
of the rector's censure would make her persist in changing
the conversation.

"Have you met young Mr Percival Haddington, Miss St
Clair? I know you are a great friend of Miss Haddington's, but
I believed her brothers had not come to visit before. It is not
easy for them, I am sure, to travel in the winter."

Judith seized on the subject, though she could not think
of what to say about her friend's brother. "He has very
engaging manners." That might have been true of Percival, at
least when he was on his first glass of wine and not his tenth.
"And his looks are a great deal like his sister's. That family
shows plenty of resemblance."

Mrs Maxwell looked up sharply at that, and Judith's father
shifted slightly in his seat. She wondered whether it was too
familiar of her to make such remarks. After all, though many
might comment on her close friendship with Louisa-
Margaretta, she did still know her face.

"Plenty of resemblance in that family," the old lady said.
"Yes, indeed, and some looks that are rather too striking
compared to what they ought to be."

"I am sure we need not speculate on their looks." Judith's
father cut off a rather large piece of his apple tart then hesitated before bringing it to his mouth. It was as if he had
meant to take his customarily small portion but forgotten.
"They are handsome, all of them. And I believe Mr Percival

Haddington's wife is an amiable woman, a great addition to the company."

Judith nearly blushed, feeling forced into one polite half-truth after another. "She is very amiable indeed. And perhaps will benefit from the society of her friends and family about her. It seems a lonely life, traveling with the army."

Mrs Barnes nodded, shifting in her seat as her little daughter lunged at the remaining tart. "Even our village can be lonely—that is, for anyone newly arrived. You seem to find companions, Miss St Clair, but would you not like to bring your sister Miriam next time? The last time I encountered her on a walk, she seemed rather out of spirits, if you will pardon me for saying so."

"The fact that she was walking at all can testify to that," Judith said. "Dear Miriam, she has always shunned any sort of exercise, though she has looked rather pale as of late."

Mrs Maxwell frowned. "Take care of your sister. A young girl with no mother, with no friends, will stray. We ought to know. My Mary was just the same."

Mrs Barnes blanched, as if hoping to avoid talk of a long-ago scandal, but she had overestimated her audience. Judith had heard nothing of a Mary Maxwell, and she would not be surprised if her father also proved ignorant of that bit of gossip. For the family, perhaps, it was still fresh, and Judith wondered if it went some way towards explaining why Mrs Maxwell lived in humble conditions. She seemed as if she had been highborn, though that might have been more a function of her sharp intellect and decided disregard for the rules of polite conversation.

The children soon provided diversion enough. It appeared one of the vanished slices of tart had been only hidden, not eaten, and there was no end to the scuffles as each child tried to retrieve that piece, all the more precious for being the last.

❧ 17 ❧

After Judith and her father said their goodbyes, they tried to stay out of the worst of the mud on their walk home. It was not more than a quarter of a mile, but even then, their boots were sure to be in a sorry state when they returned.

"It is disturbing, what they said of your sister," her father said. "I did not think her so lonely in this new situation. But then, back home she had all her friends about her. I thought that the living offered here ought not to be rejected, for various reasons that I still hold to be of the greatest import, but I certainly did not mean to injure any of my children by it."

It was, Judith thought, a particularly delicate way of speaking about money. Where her mother had been blunt— "Just think of the rich man and the eye of the needle, Judith, and be thankful that heaven will be easier for you to reach"— her father had felt that dwelling on the topic was some sort of temptation that led one towards avarice. Judith struggled not to laugh at the "various reasons" that had brought her father to his handsomely compensated position with the Haddington family.

"I am sure Miriam is not injured," she said. "We are not to let our minds be idle, as you have always said, and if she chooses not to spend her hours wisely, I do not see what more we can do about the matter."

"You will speak to her, my dear," he said, "when we get home and see how she feels. You have both been very brave since we lost your mother, and I fear it may be too much for Miriam."

Only respect for her father prevented Judith from speaking all that was in her heart. She could have told him that she was the one bearing the burden. When her father was too absent-minded to see to the household management or make sure that Moses had bothered to eat anything at breakfast—he complained terribly if he was hungry after—Judith took everything in hand. She was the one who had stepped into their aunt Leah's role, not Miriam. Miriam had perfect freedom to spend her time as she wished, which she had always enjoyed.

For a moment, she stopped to consider. If Louisa-Margaretta was dropping hints about Miriam's thoughts turning to love and matrimony, perhaps her sister felt either more happiness or more unhappiness than Judith had noticed. But she could not believe it to be so.

"Miriam," Papa said as soon as he and Judith arrived home.

She sat in the window, picking away at an old hat. If that was what she meant to wear for Easter, it was a rather sad specimen indeed. Her brothers were all outside, running about in the mud and in very great danger of getting not only sick but also shockingly filthy. Rather than minding them, she was making a terrible job of her hat.

"How are you, my dear?" He took a chair near her.

"Very well, Father," she replied with a decided want of spirits.

Judith, who had turned to see to her brothers, found herself stopped before she could leave the room.

"Judith," her father said. "Sit and chat for a moment with Miriam."

"But, Papa, the boys."

"I will see to them," he said. "It is time you two spoke."

They did not speak but watched their father as he walked outside again, in boots already muddied, to handle his sons. Instead of getting them to leave off their activities, he stood to one side, addressing them solemnly as they answered him with smiles but plainly without any intention of going back into the house.

"He won't get them to do anything," Judith said, forgetting to be cautious around Miriam.

Her sister gave a very unladylike snort. "Yes, and once they come in, he'll not convince them to wash their hands or faces either."

"Mama would have thrown at least one of them over her shoulder."

Judith thought of the way her mother used to swing all her children about. Though she had an elegant figure, she had a strength that Judith couldn't equal. Miriam would be just as strong, were she ever willing to see exercise as a pleasure rather than a punishment. Judith could only hope that she was strong enough to keep up with her brothers half the time, or Louisa-Margaretta one day a week. No matter how much she rode or walked, she never seemed to find the boundless energy of those around her. She was Mr St Clair in miniature, one of her mother's friends had said. Judith recalled that Mama had not liked that statement. Perhaps she had wished to see more of herself in Judith.

Judith cleared her throat. Gossiping with Miriam about

the young men of their acquaintance had once been a daily activity, but it felt as unnatural to her as speaking to her father about such a subject. "Miriam, you are not crossed in love, are you? Because I have observed that, ever since Mr Percival Haddington and his friends arrived, you have not been at all in good spirits."

"The soldiers?" Unlike Judith, Miriam was not in the habit of deceiving, and her surprise was plain. "An officer, turn my head? Certainly not!"

The answer was honest enough, or so Judith believed. And yet Miriam blushed, a red that crept her features, neck, and ears, and Judith knew that some truth was yet unspoken.

"It is reasonable," she said, though how any young woman could find herself taken with the soldiers was incomprehensible. Mr Green's conversation was pleasing enough, perhaps, but he was skittish, and Mr Percival Haddington might well have been a pleasant companion without the wine. Which did not signify, of course, because he was married. Mr Honor Haskett was scrupulous but also of strong opinions, which she suspected of being ill formed. The poor dead man, of course, had been both a bachelor and rather agreeable.

"Well," Miriam said. "It has not happened to me. Was that all Papa wanted to know?"

Judith bristled. She had an interest in her sister's welfare, though it had never before been as difficult as it was for her to prove that interest. "I want to know. You are not happy, and I wish you would tell me why."

"Do you?" Miriam's voice held a new note, something tremulous, not quite as bitter or as sure as the tone that had been hers even a minute ago.

"Yes," Judith said. "I do."

At that very moment, the parlor door opened, and both ladies turned away from the window to see Sally curtsy. "If you please, miss, Miss Haddington has come."

Miriam turned away so quickly Judith could not catch a glimpse of her expression, though it was plain enough from how she spoke. "Go then, to your *particular* friend."

"Miriam," Judith tried to keep the frustration from her voice, "you were about to tell me—"

"No," Miriam said, and Judith could press her no further as Louisa-Margaretta made her way towards them.

❧ 18 ❧

Louisa-Margaretta felt angry at Miss Miriam St Clair, not only for being in the way of a very important conversation but for recoiling as if Louisa-Margaretta herself were some sort of viper. True, Wycliff Castle had been mixed up in murder in a way that Miss Miriam St Clair's family had not, but that was a matter of luck, not evil. And surely the young lady remembered which family was responsible for the bread on her table. Evidently she did, for her greeting, while soft and rather late, was respectful enough.

"Is that your hat for Easter?" Louisa-Margaretta asked brightly.

"No," Miss Miriam St Clair said.

Judith, instead of being welcoming, gave her sister all manner of queer looks. "Did you come on foot?"

"Yes," she said. "The horses couldn't manage it. The road is still all mud."

Judith thought that a strong horse, such as one of Louisa-Margaretta's, could have navigated the road. But she did not say so to Miriam.

"It is rather muddy," Judith said instead. "Papa and I walked when we went to call on the Barnes family."

"I hope you found them well," Louisa-Margaretta said.

"Quite well," Miriam said quietly then said nothing else, but sat glaring at the visitor.

"In fact"—Judith gave her sister another strange look—"it was Papa and I who went, and Miriam—"

"Dear Miriam," Louisa-Margaretta interrupted. "Would you mind terribly if I asked for a private chat with your sister?"

Miriam blinked. Clearly, she had not expected such a question.

"It is most important," Louisa-Margaretta insisted. "Otherwise, I would not trouble you, of course." She walked Miriam to the door, steering her with a touch both deft and firm.

"I am not sure..." Judith said when they were alone, but her friend dragged her back to the middle of the room before she could finish the thought.

Louisa-Margaretta would not have felt any regret about hurrying the brittle little sister from the room, even if her circumstances had not been as desperate.

"I think you may have been right about Miriam," Judith said. "She seems—well, I do not quite have the words for it."

"Never mind that," Louisa-Margaretta tried to whisper but growled instead. "You must come with me. They have arrested Percival."

19

The whole way back to the house, Louisa-Margaretta nearly sank in the mud as she let Judith use her mount. It was a much more self-interested choice than it might have appeared. Louisa-Margaretta could manage mud, and Judith could nearly manage a horse. Miriam had been right to walk, as the nags her father owned would certainly have fallen. It was too wet for most horses, but Louisa-Margaretta flattered herself that this bay had better sense than most. The brilliant horse would stop and stand still rather than breaking a leg. She was smarter than most men, at least.

"But could you not tell them about your brother's character?" Judith asked, her voice despairing. "You told me yourself he hates dueling."

"I'm sure that's what all the soldiers would say," Louisa-Margaretta said, getting warmer as they walked. "And yet, one of them died in a duel."

"But surely they will release him soon. Your family's reputation—"

"Does not mean a thing to Colonel Chant. In fact, he

would like nothing better than to make an example of us. And I'm sure all that business at Christmas helps him feel that he is doing quite the right thing."

For a time, Judith did not speak, and Louisa-Margaretta was not sure whether that was due to her want of skill with horses or her ideas about the army. As they approached the house, discretion kept them both silent, though Louisa-Margaretta whispered until Judith quieted her.

"We can search the rooms the soldiers used, at least," was Louisa-Margaretta's first thought. Colonel Chant wouldn't best her. "We may yet find something that tells us what caused the duel."

Judith wrinkled her nose. "After I help you dress? You are covered in mud."

Louisa-Margaretta looked down, shaking her skirts so the largest clumps fell off. "I suppose we ought to. I've never liked this dress." She started when she saw her mother. She had not been expecting Mama quite so soon and feared having to justify her visitor.

But her mama only gave a sad smile. "Dear Miss St Clair, I am grateful you came. It will warm Mr Haddington's heart, and I am very glad to see you, my dear."

Louisa-Margaretta could not attempt to smile. "Judith has not come to warm any hearts, Mama. She will help me clear Percival's name."

"No, how could she? Pray for us, Miss St Clair. Pray that the colonel sees his error and looks into my son's heart. For he couldn't harm a soul. I am quite sure of it."

Louisa-Margaretta and her friend, after some murmurs of apology, made off for her room. Though her mother was often immersed in spiritual concerns, it was the first time Louisa-Margaretta could recall a dress as muddy as hers escaping Mama's notice.

"Mama only speaks of hearts," she said. "But how could

she claim Percival would never kill? He was going to war, and once we clear him of this charge, I am sure he shall end up in France."

Judith frowned, gingerly rolling her friend's dress as she lifted it off so the muddy part remained inside. It would not do to leave a mess on the floor if it could be avoided. "Surely it is different, though—to duel with a friend or kill a stranger in battle."

"I am sure your father would not say so."

Judith started, as if surprised that Louisa-Margaretta had come to know her father so well. But she knew the rector's family members were not allowed to speak highly of war, and from what Judith had said, her brothers were forbidden from playing at soldiers. Though, Judith had admitted, they still did it when they thought they would not be caught. "Did you ever speak with him about it?" Judith asked.

"Speak to your father about the war? He will speak to everyone about it, especially Mama. I hardly thought anything of it."

"No, speak your brother about being part of the army and having to kill."

Louisa-Margaretta rolled her eyes. "Percival doesn't give a fig for my opinion anymore. None of my brothers do. But I like him better than the others. Peggy is not nearly as intolerable as the wives the rest of them chose."

"Should we go and speak to her, then? What does she say?"

For the first time in the morning, Louisa-Margaretta was silent.

"Louisa-Margaretta? What does your sister-in-law say?"

"Nothing. She is silent. But you will see for yourself."

20

As Judith went through the house, she was impressed by both its grandeur and its order. Somehow, not even having a member of the family accused of murder could throw off Wycliff Castle's housekeeping schedule. She wouldn't have known where to find Mrs Peggy Haddington's room had Louisa-Margaretta not shown her.

"Mama liked this room for Percival," she said. "She said he would appreciate the colours."

The younger Mrs Haddington lay in her bed, looking pale. She accepted a glass of water from a trembling Harriet.

"Feeling better, Peggy?" Louisa-Margaretta asked.

She received only a slight shake of the head in reply before Mrs Peggy Haddington turned over and closed her eyes.

"We shouldn't intrude." Judith could not think what she would do if her own husband were accused of murder.

In spite of herself, she pictured being married to Mr Morgan Ramsbury and him getting jailed as a murderer. It wasn't as fanciful as it might have been. At one time, she had wondered whether he'd been involved in a murder, though even then, she had fancied him so much that she could hardly bring herself to speak of it.

"Oh, she won't mind us," Louisa-Margaretta said. "She'll be asleep soon enough. We can ask her about the soldiers when she wakes. And we can clear my brother's name while she rests."

The venom in her voice made Judith flinch. To be sure, Louisa-Margaretta had grief of her own, but it was hardly surprising that the accused man's wife was not up for running about, trying to catch a murderer.

"We just hoped for a bit of a chat," Judith said. "You see, we know little of Mr Oakley. Perhaps Mrs Haddington would know him better."

In the long pause that followed, Harriet looked about for something to occupy her hands. But the room was sparse, and apart from touching a damp cloth to the invalid's forehead, a nurse could do little.

"She knows nothing of Mr Oakley and will not be able to help us." Louisa-Margaretta sounded more tired.

Harriet looked solemn. "Sometimes, she spoke to Mr Oakley. He was a visitor."

After she spoke, she immediately coloured and looked down, but neither listener was likely to scold her for speaking out of turn.

"Yes, he came with my brother." Louisa-Margaretta looked more exasperated. "Percival's friends, those who came here, were all in the army. Nobody else would condescend to visit us here, remote as we are. Our only hope of seeing friends would be to go to London, and Mama and Papa want to keep their princess in a tower."

The bitterness in her words surprised Judith. And Harriet left, perhaps sensing that her presence was a burden as the two women stood alone by the window.

For some months, Louisa-Margaretta had seemed happier.

Though she still spoke fondly about her London home and friends, she had mostly been content to ride, shoot, and try to draw Judith into her schemes. She had even begun to say that the society of the neighborhood was just as interesting as anything she had seen in town, only one had to be a keen observer to see the scandal beneath the respectability. London, it seemed, had more public scandal.

But Judith still remembered her friend at Christmas—how she had railed against her parents, who had brought her as far from an undesirable match as they possibly could, all the while claiming publicly that they needed to be close to her father's factories in Manchester. Louisa-Margaretta had said that her father was, at times, away for months on end but that he kept his family in London so her mother would be happy. Now that they lived close to his place of business, he spent more time at home, but he did not always know how to occupy himself. Hence the building and his particularity about not only designing but also creating things that pleased him, from tables to bookshelves.

"You could leave," Judith said quietly.

Louisa-Margaretta frowned. "What, go to a different city while my brother suffers? Leave Mama and Papa to defend him while I run in cowardice?"

"After we clear his name," Judith said quickly, before her friend could accuse her of taking another's side. "If you did not wish to feel like a princess in a tower, I mean."

Louisa-Margaretta sighed. "I could go convince a man who has tired of me to make his way to Gretna Green so we could make an inadvisable alliance permanent? That is a tale of romance indeed. A sad little village where the inhabitants grow fat on ill-advised matches."

Judith knew where her friend's dislike of the place sprang from, but she thought it strange that Louisa-Margaretta had given up trying to contact her beloved. "You are strong," she said. "Stronger than I am. And I imagine you happily married without the disapproval of society touching you."

Poverty might touch her friend, though. She wondered how Louisa-Margaretta would cope. Not only had she never thought of money. She was not likely to ever have such concerns, not if she made one of the matches her parents hoped to see. Perhaps the man she hoped to marry was poor and she was biding her time, trying to get her hands on her dowry.

Louisa-Margaretta shook her head. "I cannot do such a thing. And as I said, an elopement would require a groom."

Judith touched the windowsill. The paint was perfectly even and free of dust. Despite all the mud and stink of the country, the inside of Louisa-Margaretta's large home was always immaculate.

"And the letter you sent at the end of last year?"

Judith had left off asking about it for some time, but Louisa-Margaretta's response confirmed her fears.

"I still have no response. I suppose I should not have expected one. After all, my beauty can only interest him when I am in his presence. And after no more than two months apart, he must have fallen prey to his family. I am quite sure he does not think of me now."

It was such a contrast to the picture that her friend had presented before, of being forever content as a star-crossed Heloise to her former suitor's Abelard, that Judith could talk of nothing else.

"But are you quite certain? Could not your letter have been misdirected?"

"There were two, if you will recall. So, no, despite the distance, I think they could not have been. And if he wished to write to me, he could have done so."

Louisa-Margaretta's voice had grown louder. With a glance towards the open door where Harriet had just returned, Judith steered her friend out of the room to find a place where they could speak freely. Louisa-Margaretta was tearful, but perhaps not all the tears were for her lost love. Judith knew instinctively that some of her friend's fear for Percival, trapped behind her customary bravado, might be loosed if they spoke about another man close to her heart.

By the time her tête-à-tête with Louisa-Margaretta ended, they had resolved to go to the village and seek out the soldiers. If anyone knew something that might help Percival, it would be one of his friends.

Judith, occupied with her thoughts, did not think to point out what her friend had so clearly missed earlier. Harriet, from the way she had lowered her voice when she'd spoken of Mr Oakley's visits to Mrs Peggy Haddington, had been referring to something more than a wife entertaining her husband and his friend together. In fact, there might be a great deal more taking place. But Louisa-Margaretta, impatient as she was with Harriet, had not asked. And Judith, after the moment had passed, forgot about the remark. Only later would she remember and wonder what would have happened had she thought to speak to the kind, frightened girl.

⚜ 2 1 ⚜

It was not difficult to find Mr Green. Indeed, the village was so small that Judith knew both soldiers must be nearby. Colonel Chant had gone back to Manchester, presumably to help convict Percival, but the rest of the officers were meant to stay at their station. There were other officers in town, of course, but both Judith and Louisa-Margaretta agreed that it would have been impossible for anyone to get through the flood to the dueling ground then back to the village. Too many in the village rose early and would have seen anyone slipping out of Wycliff Castle. For someone staying at the castle, on the other hand, it might be easy to slip out unobserved, which was why Mr Green and Mr Haskett were the only two individuals who would know how to clear Percival's name.

But Mr Green was not helpful at first. "Terrible thing," he said. "I like both of my fellow officers exceedingly well and cannot think how they could have come to quarrel."

Judith and Louisa-Margaretta exchanged glances. Either Mr Green was completely ignorant, or he made a rather good show of it.

"Did you ever speak of dueling?" Judith asked. "What were everyone's opinions on the subject?"

Mr Green shook his head as they walked out of the village, where a rather large branch had fallen across the road. He offered his hand first to Judith then to Louisa-Margaretta. Judith noticed that her friend gave him a grand smile and thanked him afterwards, though she needed his assistance less than Judith did.

"Oh, Mr Green," she said. "You are so kind."

At that, he finally smiled, and his shoulders visibly relaxed. "Of course, Miss Haddington. It is my pleasure."

Judith looked down at the road to compose her features.

On the walk to the village, Louisa-Margaretta had continued to talk about her struggle against the all-consuming fire of first love. No sooner has she decided to resign herself to a life that resembled Heloise's as closely as possible, both in its joy and in its misery, than she had received what she considered absolute proof that the gentleman in question had never truly cared for her. After all, if he had cared, he would have responded to her secret letter. "And it is not as if we can give a reason for his indifference," she said. "Abelard, at least, had a rather obvious cause."

Judith had laughed in embarrassment at the reference to his castration, but her heart still ached for her friend. And she felt for the first time that it was something to be part of a grand romance, even if she and Mr Morgan Ramsbury were destined never to marry. In their case, the gentleman was not at all indifferent. Of course, neither was Judith, but her affection was very greatly hindered by her duty to God and to her family.

Or just to your family, a voice whispered. *For are you confident enough in your scripture to be absolutely certain that Mr Morgan Ramsbury's life, pious as it is, could truly be displeasing to your Creator?*

As she thought of that, she nearly laughed to see Louisa-Margaretta smiling at Mr Green, then looking away. Louisa-Margaretta was such an actress. She might well feign a blush next. And Mr Green seemed completely taken in.

"Again, speaking of your brother Percival..." Judith said to Louisa-Margaretta, but she received a pointed look.

"I am sure Mr Green wishes to think of other things, does he not?" Louisa-Margaretta said.

He gave a nervous little laugh. "Well, of course I do. But you must give my love to Mr Percival Haddington. I hope this business is sorted soon."

Judith could not resist. "You could help us sort it. Did you notice anything about Mr Oakley's behavior that gave you pause? For him to get involved in a duel is a rather serious matter, and I saw nothing the evening before that made me think he had such a disagreement with any in our party."

Mr Green flinched. "In our party? Why, of course not. As I said, he was a friend to all."

Louisa-Margaretta, pausing to put her arm through Judith's and give her friend a pinch of warning, gave her best drawing room smile. "Only?"

Mr Green shifted. "Only, well, perhaps it would not be kind to say, but he——"

A figure approached them on the road, and he fell silent. Judith and Louisa-Margaretta both turned. Judith tried not to groan. It was her sister, Miriam, walking with a determination that made it clear she was not in good spirits.

$$\text{\raisebox{-2pt}{❧}} \quad 2\,2 \quad \text{\raisebox{-2pt}{❧}}$$

"Miriam," Judith said. "We did not expect you."

"I wished to go for a walk," she said. "You were not home, so I came on my own."

"Well," Judith said. "Mr Green, I know you are acquainted with my sister."

"Miss Miriam St Clair." He gave a bow that Judith found rather deep for a chance meeting. "It is a pleasure to see you here this morning. Are you paying calls in the village?"

She straightened. "Yes, in the village, and nearby. Perhaps you wish to join us? My father asked us to call on the Fletchers. Their grandmother has been ill."

Louisa-Margaretta, clutching Judith's arm, gave a peal of laughter. "Oh, their grandmother is always ill. And yet she does quite well after each illness! There have already been three rather serious alarms in our short time at Wycliff Castle."

Mr Green nodded solemnly. "This one, I am sure, may be the most serious yet. I am very little acquainted with the family."

Louisa-Margaretta and Judith looked at each other.

"I am sorry, but we cannot stop," Judith said, just as Louisa-Margaretta accepted.

"You are quite right, dear Miriam." Her smile did not quite reach her dark eyes. "It is a good while since I have seen the Fletchers, and I really ought not to neglect them. Perhaps we can all go together."

Judith walked ahead with her sister as Louisa-Margaretta told Mr Green about the family. She assumed it was the shorthand that everyone in the area used for the Fletchers, "Sweet, sour, sweet, sour, stop." With an eldest son and a third son who were both serious and kind and second and fourth sons who lived up to every kind of scandalous and impish reputation attributed to those who would not inherit, the Fletchers were an object of some fascination. Mrs Fletcher had remarried in the interim, but as her elder sons were still young when she attached herself to her second husband, they ended up taking his name.

"I do not remember when you became interested in paying calls on Papa's behalf," Judith told her sister.

Miriam looked ahead, straightening her bonnet with great dignity. "Since you were not there to take an interest, it fell to me. As many things do."

"I thought you were saving that bonnet for Easter."

"It looks very well with my eyes. I may borrow one of yours for Easter."

"Without asking?"

"Why, is there a chance you will be home? I suppose if you are, I shall ask."

Judith shook her head, but she had to admit that Miriam looked remarkably well, if perhaps a bit more energetic than was strictly appropriate if the call's purpose was to pay her respects to an elderly invalid. The bonnet did look beautiful with her eyes. Judith thought that if colours that matched Miriam's bright-blue eyes had been in fashion, they would have been set off even more favorably. As it was, Miriam mostly wore Judith's old white dresses, altered to fit her frame, as well as two new ones that their aunt Leah had insisted upon after she came out the previous winter.

"Miriam," Judith said, "I am trying to do my part for a house in mourning. I am not visiting the Haddingtons for my own amusement, you know."

"You certainly were before."

Judith coloured, remembering the very welcome attentions of Mr Morgan Ramsbury. Of late, Miriam had demonstrated more real opposition. Before, she would have contradicted Judith with her words but still recognized that some deference was due to the sister who had taken on the role of lady of the house. But recently, it was as if every attempt to guide her had become offensive.

When they reached the Fletchers and were shown into a beautiful parlor, which seemed light even on the cloudy day, Judith tried to speak with Mr Green again. It was not terribly difficult, as Louisa-Margaretta enjoyed sitting with Mrs Fletcher, whose beauty and wit were famous throughout the county. Louisa-Margaretta always had respect for ladies who could match her, no matter what their ages. She often said that if she were to be relegated to the "matrons and spinsters" corner of every party, she might as well find the wittiest of the bunch. Miriam spoke with Mr Colin Fletcher, the second son, and her laughter at his witticism was so loud and unladylike that Judith sent nervous glances their way. His older brother occupied the corner of the room, reading without the slightest regard for his company, and the younger Fletcher sons were no doubt hard at work with their tutor.

"Mr Green," Judith said, "I confess that I know little of army life. Were you acquainted with any of your current friends before you purchased your commission?"

He blinked at her. "Well, no, I was not. But then, I have

traveled a great deal and moved in many circles. If I had possessed more hours of leisure in my youth, perhaps I might have crossed paths with some of them."

Judith was puzzled. "You did not have leisurely hours in your youth, then?"

For a moment, his thin, handsome face looked strained, revealing more emotion than she had noted previously. "Many individuals in our society," he said, "including children, must search for employment, especially if they are to eat. But perhaps this necessity is foreign to you."

Judith glared at him, attempting to keep her voice down without losing track of Miriam. "I can assure you, sir, nobody in my family is ignorant of that reality. A curate father is not quite the worst hardship, but it certainly does not leave one accustomed to a life of leisure."

In no more than a moment, Mr Green's customary expression of vague solicitude returned. "I am sorry. Of course it does not. You and your sister are so refined, so carefully educated, that you would not be out of place in the best circles. Nor, I would venture to say, at court. But that made me forget myself and make assumptions about your upbringing. Please accept my apologies, Miss St Clair."

She breathed more deeply. "No apologies are needed, Mr Green."

"You are very good. But I should like to know that you accept my apology all the same. I was unpardonably rude."

"Nothing was unpardonable, and of course, I will pardon you, if that is what you demand."

"I would not presume to demand anything." He leaned closer, his voice so low it was hardly above a whisper. "But I hope to earn your good opinion again. I value it highly, Miss St Clair."

Judith feared that her face was turning pink. She had only tried to ask the man questions about his friends in the army, one of whom may well have murdered Mr Oakley, but he had turned it into an occasion for flattery. Though, she allowed, perhaps he spoke sincerely. She and Miriam would seem out of place at court, perhaps, but she would have to agree that their careful and meticulous education benefitted them in circles like the Haddintgons'.

And yet, Miriam was currently behaving outside the bounds of propriety as she sat ever so close to Mr Colin Fletcher, shooting glances at her sister that seemed both joyful and defiant. Judith decided it would be best for her to cut the visit short then have a talk with Miriam about appearing to favor one gentleman above the rest of the company. Even Mrs Fletcher had noticed, and she looked puzzled.

"Louisa-Margaretta," Judith said to her friend. "Miriam. I am afraid we must go. Our families will be expecting us."

Mr Colin Fletcher looked surprised. His brother said nothing, and their mother rose quickly.

"But of course," she said. "Thank you for coming to us. My mother-in-law does not wish to have a great deal of visitors when she is feeling poorly, and yet, that puts all of us in a rather difficult position of having to worry about her without being of any use to her. Your visit has raised our spirits."

"Indeed, it has," Mr Colin Fletcher said with great feeling.

His brother roused himself. "Thank you for visiting us."

They passed through the various niceties that the situation required, though Judith felt Miriam lingering. When the party finally left, she pushed Miriam into walking with Mr Green while she followed with Louisa-Margaretta.

❧ 23 ☙

As soon as they were certain they would not be overheard, Louisa-Margaretta asked Judith how she had fared.

"I saw you smiling at Mr Green," she said. "So, you put my ideas to work after all! What did he say?"

Judith lowered her head. She did not like to think how Mr Green's words had affected her. After Mr Morgan Ramsbury had left, she at least had enough pride to say that she had not felt any bit of genuine interest for another man. And yet she could not help wondering why Mr Green desired her good opinion so highly.

"That he grew up poor," she said carefully, "and he thought Miriam and I must be rich and frivolous. He apologized for that. But he had nothing else to contribute to the conversation."

"Could he have wanted Mr Oakley dead because the man was rich?"

"If so, he would hardly have admitted that contempt to me. Though he seemed unguarded, if it were his reason for murder, I am sure he would not simply let it slip."

Judith worried that she was making the whole matter too simple. Even then, she watched Miriam and Mr Green closely from where she stood, both to present an appearance of a close and attentive chaperone and to be sure she had not just thrust her sister onto the arm of a murderer.

"If only we did not have to contrive these awkward meetings," Louisa-Margaretta said. "All of the soldiers were happy to speak when Percival was plying them with wine. But Mama says we cannot have any of them dine with us under the circumstances, and I rather think she is right."

"Well, given we have no other way of meeting them, we may as well admit that we shall discover nothing useful," Judith said, though Louisa-Margaretta seemed loathe to agree.

"We haven't found anything useful yet," she said. "Everyone is too distracted to speak. And it's not as if any of the soldiers will be eager to confess what they know."

Judith shuddered. "Suppose it was not one of them? The murderer could be anywhere in the neighborhood."

"I'm not so sure it counts as murder if it was a duel at any rate." Louisa-Margaretta attempted to fix her bonnet while gazing around the village, as if a mirror would magically appear before her. "I'm not even sure why we are in mourning for Mr Oakley. We barely knew him, and this accusation against Percival makes it all rather awkward."

"How can you be so unfeeling? This is your brother," Judith could not help saying, aggravated by the sight of Louisa-Margaretta twisting her gold-and-pearl earring to make it even with its match.

Her friend turned to her, apparent indifference turning to fury in no more than a moment. "Of course I am not unfeeling! Though I have no idea why moping about would make me seem more attached to Percival. I bring not smelling salts but a sword."

"I'm sorry." Judith shrank back before approaching her friend again. "Truly, I am. Only I didn't manage anything, and we are just as ignorant as we were before. I feel that your faith in me is misplaced."

Louisa-Margaretta turned away, and Judith thought she caught a sniff and a curious movement of her friend's wrist.

But when Louisa-Margaretta turned back, her cheeks were dry, her eyes flashing in the muted spring light that filtered between the clouds. "It is not misplaced. You are a genius, and I am widely believed to be a fool. Between us, we will find out which soldier it was."

When Judith was silent, Louisa-Margaretta amended her statement. "Fine, or which other man did it, though I am quite sure it was a soldier. The trouble is that nobody will speak to us in a house of mourning, and it is no better if we wander the village looking grim. That parlour we just left was even worse. It was so quiet, and though I do love Mrs Fletcher dearly, anything said in her hearing will be halfway around the village before evening."

"I'm not sure what choice we have," Judith said. "If your family were to come out of mourning, the scandal would be greater. And where can we go besides the village?"

Louisa-Margaretta smiled wickedly. "Oh, we need only a few card tables and some wine. I said it moments ago, and I know that I am right. Everyone will speak at a party."

$\maltese$ 24 $\maltese$

Judith, who believed Lent was no time for parties, thought her friend could not be right. Certainly it would be unseemly for the Haddingtons themselves to hold any sort of gathering while their son stood accused of murder.

But the charming Miss Haddington worked her magic on one neighborhood family. Mr Colin Fletcher, as they had seen the day before, was perennially eager for both company and cards. That was enough for Louisa-Margaretta. And as she often did, the dowager made a rather rapid recovery from her ailment. Judith wondered whether her "illness" was imagined, though she dared not say so before her father, who had his own views on the connection between illness of the spirit and corresponding maladies of the body.

Before Judith could count the days, they both sat in beautifully embroidered chairs at a small and tasteful gathering. Several local families, along with the soldiers, attended, though Colonel Chant's absence was conspicuous. Judith hoped it was because he was not yet sure of Mr Percival Haddington's guilt, though she acknowledged it might well be due to a reluctance to attend social gatherings with his soldiers.

Mr Haskett sat iron-rod straight at one of the tables, and both their host and his eldest son looked hardly more cheerful. The table was only made more interesting by the presence of one Miss Lockton, a neighbor Judith had never much noticed before. Though she would never have Louisa-Margaretta's fortune, she was the second-richest young lady in the neighborhood, which made her the object of some interest. But if Mr Fletcher hoped to encourage his eldest son, he was having very little success. And the young Mr Colin Fletcher hardly took his eyes off his cards.

Judith gave her friend a timorous smile as they found a small sofa where their conversation would not be overheard.

"What is our aim, then?" she asked. "I am sure neither Mr Green nor Mr Haskett is particularly interested in conversing with me."

"Oh, you need not speak to them," Louisa-Margaretta said. "Only join the general conversation. If you ignore them a bit, they will surely seek your attention."

Judith winced, which made her friend give her wide, true smile for the first time since the ordeal began.

"Oh, Judith, surely you can manage such a thing. Though your face says you will hate it."

"It seems like the sort of stratagem often given to young ladies," Judith managed. "And I have never had success with that."

"You had success enough with dear Cousin Morgan," her friend said. "Perhaps I should invite him for a visit. It will give you more practice, and I shall have the satisfaction of seeing you blush."

Judith sighed. "What is your aim, then?" she asked feebly, hoping her friend would leave her to her thoughts.

"I will talk with Peggy." Louisa-Margaretta sighed.

"Though I doubt it will do much good. Mama has tasked me with keeping her from jumping out a window."

"Surely she would not," Judith said, surprised that her friend could joke about such an eventuality, especially when the accused's wife seemed to display a calm that rivaled Louisa-Margaretta's.

They both looked at Mrs Peggy Haddington, who spoke to Mrs Fletcher, her hands folded delicately in her lap. She looked a bit pale but nearly emotionless.

"Well," Louisa-Margaretta said, "she has either completely lost her wits, or she is doing a very good job of her Daniel-in-the-lion's-den charade."

Judith frowned. She did not love to hear beloved Bible tales used to describe the way ladies behaved in society. Then again, she wondered if Mrs Peggy Haddington held as much terror in her heart as ever Daniel did. Peggy might hear any day that her husband was to die, and her humiliation would surely endure. Judith had to wonder if even Louisa-Margaretta's mother, with all her talk of souls and ever-present godliness, could bear to keep a daughter-in-law who would be a daily reminder of the deepest stain on the family's honor.

"There are the boys," Judith said as the younger Fletchers made their way into the room, followed at a rather great distance by a nurse who looked more harried than stern. The older of the pair chased the younger, who held two books over his head.

"Darling," Mrs Fletcher said, "do give him the books back. Come here."

Her orders were not at all effective, but she did leave Mrs Peggy Haddington's side, and her place was taken by both her second son and Miriam. Mr Colin Fletcher gestured for Mr Green and Mr Haskett to join them, and Judith saw her chance.

The conversation centered primarily not around naughty

children but rather the festivities they were to expect after Easter.

"Why should we wait for May to be joyful?" Mr Colin Fletcher gazed about him.

Judith detected a hint of a blush on Miriam's face. She realized that, just as it was never easy to tolerate their neighbors' sacrilegious comments, even Miriam must struggle to remain observant for their father's sake.

"You would have us be joyful now?" Mrs Peggy Haddington's hands grew tighter in her lap.

If there was a hint in her tone, Mr Colin Fletcher refused to hear it. "Why, yes. We should not only eat the very best food before Lent but also immediately after. Why should we lose a day's pleasure once the season of eating dry cakes and pathetic little suppers is over?"

Mr Green nodded slowly. "Perhaps the weather here does not quite lend itself to such celebrations, sir."

Mr Honor Haskett shrugged. "Some of us have no time for such celebrations at any rate."

Mr Colin Fletcher smiled a bit. "Surely the rector's daughters have something to say. Miss Judith St Clair, Miss Miriam St Clair, what are your opinions?"

Miriam broke in, smiling, before Judith could. "I think you are quite right. At least we ought to take more time to celebrate Easter."

"That depends on our inclinations, surely." When Mrs Peggy Haddington received no response, she said, "You must excuse me."

$$ \text{25} $$

As Judith left the room behind Louisa-Margaretta's sister-in-law, she found herself wondering if Mrs Peggy Haddington had taken several glasses of wine. The lady's gait became quite unsteady, and Judith had to help her into a drawing room, where they hardly made it to a sofa.

Peggy's breathing was much too fast. It was as if she could not draw air, but was determined to try, and her head began to loll to one side. Her eyes were wide open but unseeing.

"I will pray for you," Judith burst. She was not her father in such situations, but she did know to use prayer when she could think of nothing else. She began the prayer as if it were all one thought, nearly one word. "Our father who art in heaven hallowed be thy name thy kingdom—" She broke off when she noticed Mrs Peggy growing worse. "Whatever is the matter?" she asked, though of course she knew. "Could I help you to the window? Perhaps the night air."

Poor Mrs Peggy Haddington's breathing was still alarmingly fast. It reminded Judith of the time Aaron had nearly stopped breathing as a baby. In fact, he had stopped breathing, many times. Miriam had started to cry, and Judith had run for her father, but their mother had stayed calm. She'd used the night air and songs to calm the child. Judith had no idea what stratagem she might employ to calm her friend's sister-in-law, but she was given one just in time.

"These stays are too tight," Mrs Peggy Haddington managed. "I don't care what anyone says about the new fashions. No corset could have tortured me so. It is Tattershall's fault. Go find her."

"I am here, madam," Tattershall said, though Judith could not remember seeing her come in. "Please leave it to me."

Tattershall redid the stays and the way the dress sat. Because it was black, it did not show how loose the stays were, not when Mrs Peggy Haddington was covered in her shawl. They might have fallen off. Peggy sank onto the sofa, her head lowering into the cushions, and she seemed to lose track of both Judith and Tattershall. It seemed much kinder not to wake her, though the little card party was hardly the sort of place where a guest ought to fall asleep.

Judith shifted in her chair, eager to return to the gathering before they were missed but knowing that she could hardly leave. At least Tattershall's presence would mean nobody could accuse her of being truly unchaperoned. Even the lady who had fainted on the sofa could be considered her chaperone. Whatever her circumstances, Mrs Peggy Haddington at least had the advantage of a respectable marriage.

Judith opened the door to the hall. It was mostly silent, but she caught a glimpse of Mr Haskett and Mr Green.

"I told you that I wouldn't tell anyone," Mr Haskett said. "You have my word, and you ought to know I would not break it."

"But what price am I to pay for this silence?" Mr Green asked. "And what price are you forcing others to pay if you say nothing?"

Mr Haskett made some sort of reply, and Judith thought it contained the word "prove," but she could not be sure.

That was all they said before they were out of sight. Judith wished to follow them, but she felt she could not leave the poor woman sleeping in the drawing room. If she was very careful, she might manage to wake the young Mrs Haddington and prepare her for company before their absence became unreasonably long.

When she went back in, she saw Tattershall must have had the same instinct. The maid was already preparing a handkerchief and smelling salts.

"Thank you," Judith said to the lady's maid. She wondered if Tattershall could be compared to the woman from the children's song "London Bridge" and tried to remember the story. *Was there not one legend saying a lady-in-waiting for a poor beheaded queen was the "fair lady" in that song? Would Tattershall stay with her mistress, even if it meant consoling a woman whose husband had been killed in the most brutal and public manner imaginable?*

Tattershall only nodded. "It is my duty."

"I cannot imagine," Judith said. "I wish to offer sympathy, and yet, I have no sense of what she feels." She knew she should not unburden herself to Tattershall, but she was so sick with emotion for the young woman before her that she hardly knew what to say. "It is cruel," Judith continued, "when a couple is torn apart in this way. Surely what each wants most is the other's company and counsel, and that is just what is denied them."

Tattershall did not speak, and Judith collected herself.

"I am sorry," she said. "Only I am not well acquainted with either of them. Perhaps I imagine more than what I see before me."

Tattershall nodded. "I should not say this, but theirs was not an untroubled marriage."

Judith tried not to give any indication that she found that

piece of information interesting. "Well, of course they were newly married. And young."

She felt rather odd saying it. *What could I, a spinster who does not even have the wisdom of age on my side, know of such things?* But she often heard that the honeymoon was the cruelest time and the first years of a marriage less than easy. She had even gotten such indications from her mother, though Mama had always said that baby Judith had made her journey into living as a curate's wife an easier one.

Tattershall set down the handkerchief. "If I may say so, my lady has always had nothing on her mind but children. And it is cruel that she cannot bear one of her own."

Judith knew better than to ask for details, but she had also known that her father was a particular advocate for caring for all children, not just children with whom one shared blood. Whenever a child was in need in his parish, he found a place for them—often not with distant relatives but with strangers who would offer a warmer and more welcoming home. He disliked the practice of sending children to relatives who were not loving. They had neighbors who cared for a young cousin of theirs, one from a large and impoverished family several villages away. Her father had hated to see the boy set apart from his cousins.

"They ought to treat them all the same," he'd said again and again until Mama had put one hand over his.

"Not all God's creatures can be as kind as you are, dear," she'd said.

"Perhaps," Judith said quietly, "they could find a child to care for. Perhaps even if it is not their natural child."

Tattershall nodded. "I believe that would do for her, but he thinks differently."

She did not need to explain that. Judith only nodded, and Mrs Peggy Haddington stirred. After some smelling salts as well as a turn about the room, Judith helped the other woman back the drawing room.

And all the while she thought about Mr Percival Haddington, a man who refused the one action that would have brought joy to his miserable young wife. *Surely, the desire to make him pay for her unhappiness would not cause Mrs Peggy Haddington to do something so mad as shooting his friend to frame him for the murder?* Judith was certain the woman leaning on her arm was genuinely distressed. *Is that because she seeks the identity of a murderer or because she already knows it?*

❧ 26 ☙

L ouisa-Margaretta rose early, which was not like her. She could not wait long to hear what her friend had to say, but she knew it would seem suspicious if she went to Judith's right away.

So, instead, she sat with her mother for an hour, which was torture. Dear Mama spent all her time either praying or choosing the prayer that would come next in her frantic pleas for her son's life. Louisa-Margaretta could not remember half the prayers or verses her mother had tasked her with memorizing, but Mama hardly seemed to notice she only mumbled along part of the time.

When she was summoned to meet Judith, her spirits lifted at last. There would be no walk to the rectory. Her friend had come to call on her instead. She was eager to share what she had learned from the evening before.

"I'm sure you heard the news," she told Judith, licking her lips. It was a relief to remember that she could care for something besides her brother's troubles.

Judith hesitated, looking around the hall.

"Oh, everyone knows," Louisa-Margaretta said, but she called for her coat anyway.

As soon as she and Judith were a distance from the house, she burst out with it. "Mr Colin Fletcher is engaged! Of course, it should not come as a surprise, for he is vain and as silly as anything and must have something to live on. But to think of him and Miss Lockton! They never showed a bit of interest in each other before now. At least, I am sure he did not care for her at all. And they had plenty of opportunities for meeting in town during the season, so I must believe that if there were any true regard, they would not have waited until they were back in our neighborhood."

Judith shook her head. "Indeed, I did not hear."

"But everyone was congratulating them!"

"Your sister-in-law was barely breathing. And by the time we got back to the drawing room, Miriam was in a temper about something, and we had to leave. Though I am sure I did see Mrs Fletcher with Miss Lockton. She looked rather happy, if I remember it."

"Which one? Both, I'm sure. Mrs Fletcher to get that son of hers off her hands. It will be just the same with the youngest. Well, and what did you learn, then?"

Judith frowned, her steps slowing. Louisa-Margaretta tried to keep herself from shouting. For someone who could issue very precise descriptions, Judith always seemed loathe to describe anything she had observed. It was as if she believed God listened to her every word. Louisa-Margaretta had never been scared by the prospect, not even in the nursery. If God did exist, surely her mother's words would drown out anything she herself had to say. *And,* she reflected wryly, *God is not doing a very excellent job for Himself if He won't see Percival released very soon.* She had always thought her mother's faith completely unshakeable. Still, despite everything that had happened before her family had buried her in

Derbyshire, not to mention the unpleasant business at Christmas, perhaps that faith had never been tested quite like it was currently.

"Judith," Louisa-Margaretta said, "you were gone with Peggy for some time. Tell me what she told you! She knows both Mr Green and Mr Haskett better than anyone, and neither of them was very forthcoming."

Judith stared off at the lake, not meeting Louisa-Margaretta's eyes. "She was not the one who spoke with me. It was her maid."

"Even better! Of course Tattershall would know. Well, what was it?"

"Their marriage is troubled."

Louisa-Margaretta would have laughed, had she not snorted. "Yes, Percival can be unbearable. Though Peggy ought to bear up better. Haddingtons do not fare well with weak wives."

Judith frowned. "Surely that is not fair. Perhaps your sister-in-law is not the strongest woman, but she is enduring such a trial. As are you."

Louisa-Margaretta could not bear the sympathetic hand that flew to her shoulder, and she shook it off. "Yes, well, I do not see what bearing their marriage has on anything. If you are speaking of Percival's physical defect, I have no intention of discussing it, except to say that his wife has always known very well that he cannot possibly be a father. Could you not learn more from Tattershall?"

Judith nodded. "You just told me you do not wish to hear it, but what she said was that your sister-in-law wants a child and that your brother will not accept raising a child that is not his own."

Louisa-Margaretta shook her head. "Well, I'm sure she could convince him. And besides, that has very little to do with Mr Oakley."

Judith was silent for so long that Louisa-Margaretta finally glared at her. "Well, and so you think it does. What is it, then? My sister-in-law wanted to bear Mr Oakley's child, and Percival shot him rather than see himself a cuckold? Or Peggy was so angry that she wanted Percival to die, so she learned how to shoot and conjured a duel from thin air? She couldn't shoot a chicken if I held it up in front of her. Honestly, I don't know where you could conceive of such mad ideas."

Judith's face fell. "Please, Louisa-Margaretta. I did not say anything of the sort."

"You did not need to. The fact that you can think it, can imply it, speaks loudly enough."

"But I did not mean to offend you! What I meant—"

"What you meant can have no bearing. I hope you go back to your family. Go, find out why Miriam was in a temper. Perhaps it is because she must share a household with a sister who has mad visions and betrays her friends at every turn."

Judith let out a sort of whimper, but Louisa-Margaretta was already striding away. She would find a horse. She would ride. She would not turn around until she was well into the hills. And she would certainly never speak to Judith again.

❧ 27 ❦

Louisa-Margaretta had hardly known what she was doing when she took the horse. The weather was still unpleasant, not quite rainy but certainly damp. It was cold, and the hints of spring she had observed seemed entirely lost beneath her black mood.

Only when she started riding did she realize her destination. The morning Mr Oakley was killed, she and Judith had been the ones to find him, and she was trying to remember that. Perhaps she had missed something then or might discover something after a second look that could lead her to the real murderer.

As she rode, she could not keep thoughts of Percival from invading her head. Judith was generally a rather good judge of character, except when it came to the way she fawned over Mr Ramsbury. *All that talk of elopement!* Judith, who surely had no fortune of her own, ought to be the one eloping. Louisa-Margaretta did not understand why she could not just go to Gretna Green herself and have done with it. As if there were any great scandal in being a nonconformist or in marrying one. Judith herself could keep going to services every bit as staid and quiet as her father's of a Sunday, and Cousin Morgan could go to those strange meetings he enjoyed. If Judith knew the first thing about men, Louisa-Margaretta thought, she would not have passed up such a good match without at least considering it.

But outside the little matter of her possible engagement, Judith could often tell when a person was not to be trusted. The jewels and titles of society did little to sway her. So perhaps, if Judith believed Percival to be guilty...

But Louisa-Margaretta could not bear the thought. The young woman who had, until an hour ago, been her closest friend, could not possibly understand what had happened. Louisa-Margaretta had felt throughout that they did not yet comprehend something about the duel. A group of young men did not simply gather in a fine house, have a horrible, meagre supper from a hostess who insisted on feeling God's presence in every thin spoonful, then decide to kill each other. If one of them had done it, they must have had some motive beyond the terse table conversation. And perhaps the place where the murder had occurred would show her.

It was only once she arrived at the clearing and dismounted that she realized she might have gone alone to a dangerous place. The clearing was not close to the house, and she wondered whether anything she said there would be heard by someone so far away. Nobody had reason to come to that part of the grounds in spring. Sensing another's presence, Louisa-Margaretta turned back towards her horse, but by then, she had already gone a hundred paces, and she knew that she might not outrun the person who had arrived there before her.

"Who's there?" She despised the fear in her voice but could not manage to say anything else.

Then she saw him, and he was much closer than she would have believed. She turned to run.

"**M**iss Haddington, I am sorry." Mr Green held his hands in front of him in a gesture of supplication.

"I did not know you were here." She tried to force courage back into her voice. Perhaps only the anger came across.

"I hope I have not offended you," he said. "It is your father's land, I know. Only today I wished—"

"You should leave," she said. "Quickly."

"And so I shall." He spoke more eagerly. "But I must know that I have not offended you first. Please, speak to me."

"Why would I speak with you, Mr Green? What on earth is so urgent that we must speak now, here, in this place?" She could not bring herself to speak any more directly of the murder. The fear she had felt a moment ago still choked her. She had been thinking of the whole thing as little more than a game until that moment.

"Please, do not force me to be eloquent." The man rose to walk after her.

"Do not follow me," she said, and he stopped immediately.

Louisa-Margaretta, in her heart, believed that she would have made an excellent queen or empress. In fact, when she played with her brothers, she liked to take on the titles of famous regents. *What was the trouble with ruling in the stead of a husband or son, as long as one did it well?* Catherine the Great of Russia was one of her favourites. So, when Mr Green obeyed her, it made her willing to listen. Before she mounted her horse, she turned back. She would give him one moment.

"You are the sister of one of my dearest friends, and you are very beautiful, if you will permit me to say it." He lowered his eyes as he spoke.

He said it while only asking for permission afterwards, but she nodded. "Go on, then."

"If it were not imprudent"—he swallowed—"I would ask for your hand. But I have nothing to offer you, and I know your parents would not approve."

She blinked, worried for the first time. "Then, what are you proposing?"

He took her meaning immediately. "Only to admire you from afar. I will do everything I can to help your parents and your brother."

The omission of her sister-in-law was curious but not one that Louisa-Margaretta could fault. She had been so angry with Peggy of late that she could hardly consider her part of the family.

"Can you tell us nothing that will help him?" she asked. "Surely, you of all people must know what would have brought Mr Oakley to duel."

Mr Green raised his hands. "It is as incomprehensible to me as it is to you. Though I am a soldier, I have never approved of dueling. It is foolish to risk one's life for what is often the flimsiest of reasons."

"What do you know of Mr Oakley's reasons?"

"Nothing, I assure you." He paled. "Only that I cannot imagine they were worth the sacrifice."

Louisa-Margaretta mounted her horse, wondering if he was telling the truth. "Goodbye, Mr Green."

"Miss Haddington." He blushed again. "I hope you are not offended?"

"No," she said with little hesitation. "Though, of course, I would appreciate it if you did not speak of this to anyone."

"Of course, of course," he said as she rode away.

It was only once she was out of his sight that she allowed herself a smile. So, another proposal, after all that. Plenty of gentlemen in the neighborhood had not been entirely secret about the fact that they would be quite happy to find a rich wife. However, Louisa-Margaretta's manner had always been enough to make it clear that they need not bother asking for her hand, as she would not be inclined to give it. That made Mr Green either very brave or very stupid.

Reflecting on his blushes and how she had startled him in the clearing, she did not find him particularly brave. She hoped that the pleasant hint of romance his attentions brought would not be outweighed by her natural disapproval of anyone who was not her equal in strength. She had respected Judith, of course, but that was only because Judith's naturally pious timidity was balanced by a stubborn yearning for justice that made her both canny and courageous.

Just then, the desire to tell Judith about what had just transpired came over her, but she fought the impulse. She would tell nobody. Judith was disloyal, eager to decide that Percival was a murderer. Then she would not have to do the work of finding the real culprit.

Louisa-Margaretta tried to think through what she had learned. It was entirely up to her to find the other party in the duel. But her mind kept going back to Mr Green's offer of marriage. She knew from Isaac's silence that she would not find happiness in matrimony. So, perhaps, she ought to find a tolerable husband who would not expect a great deal from her. She could easily imagine herself running a household and telling Mr Green exactly what to do and how to behave.

Mr Green had said that her parents would not approve. On that point, Louisa-Margaretta reflected, he was not entirely correct. Her parents were so eager to find a less unsuitable husband for her than the one she had found for herself, they would surely approve. Whatever else Mr Green was, he was a gentleman and a Christian, and perhaps they would set their sights low enough for that to suffice. She was quite sure they would not want her to be a burden on any of her brothers.

If only Judith had been willing to sell music with her. Then, perhaps, she need not be a burden on anyone. As long as she remained without any money of her own, she would face down a cold and uncertain future as a none-too-devoted aunt at some miserly brother's fireside. She had always thought that Percival and Peggy would have a better home than most if she had to live as an old spinster with no money, but those prospects looked none too good.

It was not the kind of romance she had dreamed of, the sort that she privately expected as her due. After all, even if money were a consideration, she always thought she could blind herself to such a thing. A young man, rich or poor, would fall in love with her, and her rather ample fortune would ensure that he did not love in vain.

Instead, she found herself just as rich but heartbroken. And if she was only to have money on her marriage, then her surest way to independence might be to tie herself to some man.

Gripping the reins tighter, she hurried back to the house, a plan forming in her mind. She could not make such a decision until Percival's name was cleared. If she managed to find proof of his innocence, she would allow her life to begin again. She would insist on going back to town with one of her brothers and threaten her parents if they tried to stop her. If she were to save Percival, after all, they could hardly ask any more of her.

If she could not prove Percival's innocence, she would marry Mr Green and escape her family in that way. She could not allow herself to think of what would happen if she did not clear Percival's name and the army decided that he was guilty of his friend's death. But she imagined a sort of purgatory in which he was still suspected yet never hanged and the killer walked free. He would have his life but little else, and her family would have only shame. This outcome seemed likely unless she did something.

She shivered as she dismounted and went back towards the house with long strides. Searching every room had felt impossible when Judith first proposed it, but she would have to do it. Surely one of them could tell her something of Mr Oakley.

❦ 29 ❦

They came by stagecoach because Judith's father had insisted. The Haddingtons had offered their coach, and she knew it would have been complete with warm cloaks and hot-water bottles as well as a generous hamper from the cook. But her father's response forbid her from begging.

"It would be faster, Papa," she insisted. "We may not even reach the barracks until nearly dark."

"We have no reason to ask for charity," he said, "especially from a family who has already given so much. We can be certain of a warm welcome at the Cliftons'."

Judith tried to ignore the implications. Her father did not want to ask for charity from the Haddingtons, but surely that was a formality. As he had rightly pointed out, the Haddingtons had provided them with their home and income. *So, what suspicions must he harbor if he hesitates to accept even a carriage ride?* Manchester was not far, and the journey would have been much faster if they did not have to stop every few miles to take on some passengers and allow others to leave. The cost to

Wycliff Castle if they took one of the Haddingtons' coaches, though considerable, would be trifling when placed next to all the other things they had received from that family.

She also did not like the sound of the Cliftons. If they were anything like their Brackenfield cousins, they would be noisy and eager for any tidbit of gossip about the accused.

"Tell me again why these Cliftons will welcome us." She counted the buds on a nearby bush as they waited for the coach to be ready, wishing she could at least be out of the wind, even without a hot-water bottle.

One old man had come out of the inn to rap on the wheels with his cane, much to the coachman's chagrin. "Good wheels, these," the old man said. "Unbroken iron!"

"Please, sir. Our passengers are waiting."

"When I was a lad, a rock could take down a bigger wheel than this. Nails and scraps, that's all a wheel was."

"Sir, begging your pardon," the coachman said to Mr St Clair. "If you and the lady would like to come aboard."

Mr St Clair nodded as the coachman glared at the old man, who was not in the least put out by the fact that he was impeding the passage of two weary travelers.

"We will depart shortly." The coachman placed one hand on the old man's back and another on his elbow as he attempted to clear a path.

Judith sat far along the bench, though the small window was high above her head. The coach, like the yard, stank of manure and horses. It seemed the coachman had been rather quick to usher them in, as it was some minutes before they began. The silence that usually overcame inhabitants of a stagecoach was upon Judith, and she feared that speaking directly about Percival would be indiscreet with the coachman and his boy so close. The old man also kept banging on about the carriages of his youth, at least until a young woman came out of the inn and took him away with none of the coachman's gentle manners.

She sat quietly, wondering if Louisa-Margaretta would ever speak to her again. Though her friend was a great one for threats and dramatics, when she had sworn that she would not speak with Judith, she had seemed absolutely serious. And Judith, in her ignorance, had done something unforgivable. She had implied that Mr Percival Haddington might, in fact, be guilty of the charge laid before him. Lousia-Margaretta would never forgive an accusation like that, no matter its basis. It must be a stark reminder that Judith, no matter how fond she was of the Haddingtons, was not part of the family.

Started on the road was a balm. Judith could convince herself that, by sitting in a moving carriage, she was doing more for her friend than she had been simply standing on the hard ground, waiting to set out on the journey. "Father," she said, "do you think Percival Haddington is guilty?"

He turned away. In a carriage that was supposed to seat eight to a dozen passengers on each bench but only held two at that moment, he could not escape the question. "It is not my place, child. Rather, it is not our place to judge Percival Haddington."

"Mama would have said, 'Well, I'll make it my place, and a very good place it will be, too.'" Judith never could have said such a thing to her father directly, but she was gratified to see that the remembrance of her dear mama's voice made him laugh. "It may be our place to serve Mr Haddington, surely," she continued. "And how are we to serve him if we do not know whether he was part of this duel?"

He nodded. "He is a sinner, my dear. The nature of his sin is not the only matter of import, but rather, the sincerity of his repentance."

Judith nodded, hardly listening. "Will we ask him?"

"We are not his confessors, my dear. God is his confessor."

"True," Judith mused. "We are hardly Papists."

He smiled. "Hardly, my dear. But as you know, no one faith has sole ownership of truth or of God."

He could not have been sensible of the pain his words caused her, and she was thankful when the stagecoach shuddered to a halt and an elderly woman boarded with her daughter. Their greetings were perfunctory, so Judith took the opportunity to lean her head against the carriage wall and feign sleep.

She could picture the countryside around them. Hills with bursts of green, clouds with whispers of sunlight. Though she had complained that spring would never come to the north, of course it must, and she noticed enough buds to remind her that warmth and flowers would eventually follow. Though perhaps it would be long after Lady Day.

Sleep would not come. Her father's thoughts, spoken musingly in an easy moment, would not release her. She had never thought her father's church held the only truth. *How could it, when so many texts of different faiths are the same?* Any of the sermons he made about his sons' and daughters' namesakes could very nearly have been made in a synagogue, for he was exceedingly fond of the Old Testament Mr St Clair, as a curate then a vicar and now a rector, had always loved the earlier books of the Bible best.

Mr Morgan Ramsbury remained the only gentleman of her heart. She could not have said whether he was the most learned, the most amiable, or even the most pious, but he surely was all those things and so handsome that she longed for him still.

Judith heard Louisa-Margaretta's words about how such longing could be a comfort, a protection from other entanglements and the many disadvantages that even the most prudent marriage could hold for a young lady.

But she had a time believing them. She could not think herself happier for having known Mr Ramsbury's affections—or for having been very nearly the recipient of his marriage proposal, which she was quite sure would have followed his confession of being a nonconformist had her reaction not preempted such an offer.

A nonconformist. She had always found the term laughably mild—to go against one's upbringing, one's family, one's king and country. Though perhaps, she reflected, not so much against the king himself. *May the good Lord bless him with health,* she prayed, not least because even the most enthusiastic sycophant could not convince her that the prince regent was a worthy man. In truth, she often wished him ill and had to pray all the more fervently to make up for that.

No matter how she tried to wrest her thoughts from the ghost of Mr Ramsbury's grasp, they tormented her. And she searched them for signs that Mr Ramsbury did not conform, rifling through them as she would a beloved book, the pages worn with age and rereading.

When they had first met, it was very nearly Christmas, and she had regaled him with a tale from her girlhood. She wondered whether she ought to have known then, though she had been rather more wrapped up in his gaze and her memories than in any serious contemplation of his words.

Her father had been curate and caretaker to a cantankerous old vicar whom nobody much liked. Even as a child, Judith was polite to Mr Lewis, but after Miriam began to speak, her mother had a time keeping her from questions like "Why Mr Lewis mean?" and "Mr Lewis eat. Mana no eat. Why Mr Lewis eat?"

For he did eat with their parents from time to time and seemed to take special care to serve himself unreasonably large portions of each dish, forcing everyone else at the table to politely accept small scraps. As he had been more than happy to turn over all his duties to the young, underpaid Mr St Clair, those meals were one of the only times she saw him. Christmas was the other time.

"Good evening, friends, neighbors, and occasional church-goers." His voice, high-pitched and querulous, nevertheless carried well across a crowd swollen with many who attended but rarely.

A hearty note of laughter followed. It was rare for Mr Lewis to make a joke, rarer still for the crowd to be appreciative.

He brought his large hands together in front of his chest, peering into the crowd as if to catch anyone who had dared to laugh. "That was not a joke."

And Mr Lewis, who never wrote his own sermons, proceeded that night to read a tract of his own creation. It was less comprehensible than the sermons from any book Judith had ever seen and much longer. It contained not a single allusion to the season or even to Jesus himself—much less the Christ child.

Waves of uneasiness swept over the crowd. Judith was tasked with keeping Miriam quiet, which she did by whispering about the treats to come. When even that failed, Mana took the child out the door, away through the cold night to their little home.

Judith couldn't remember how the sermon ended, as she fell asleep on the pew. The first services of the new year were notable for their very poor attendance. If Mr Lewis's aim was to play on his parishioners' guilt and drive them to his young curate's services that way, he had failed. If his aim was to terrify them, perhaps he had succeeded.

Of course, all the families who had spoken to young Mr St Clair were quick to assure him that they had missed church due to the depth of the snow, not their feelings about Mr Lewis.

"I wonder what they would have said to Mr Lewis," Mr Ramsbury had said after she'd told him.

They were looking out at the snow themselves. The two of them were supposed to be having tea with Mrs Haddington and Louisa-Margaretta, but the latter had begged her mother's assistance with some snarls in her workbasket. Judith, who knew her friend despised any task that required sitting still like a proper young lady, was thankful for the interlude.

"Nobody ever spoke to Mr Lewis," she said. "He talked with his patrons, but not with his parishioners."

"That is precisely the trouble," Mr Ramsbury said, warming to the topic. "How could he ask his neighbors to join him in a place where their voices were not respected, where they must be always silent?"

Judith paused. It was not so very different from her father's church. While he respected his parishioners deeply, it was not as if they had opportunities to speak to him on Sundays. At least not until the formal bit was over and he stood at the door, eager to wish them well before they went back to their hearths.

"For some, the singing is enough." She had wondered, at the time, what Mr Ramsbury had been driving at. Surely it would be strange for anyone apart from the clergyman to speak.

She no longer had to wonder about that.

Her image of the "meetings" that Mr Morgan Ramsbury attended was a dark one. She remembered hearing one of his aunts ask him about one such gathering. He had stammered and run off in reply. Judith had in her mind an image of a dark space, with men and women together, dressed in a strange fashion. Though Mr Morgan Ramsbury's clothes during his stay with the Haddingtons had not been conspicuously plain, neither had he been fond of those bright colours and fine fabrics that defined the dress of every other man except Louisa-Margaretta's father. But she imagined him wearing something akin to sackcloth, the ladies in formless dresses that were hardly better than dark shifts.

And to think that all the men and women spoke whenever they felt moved! To Judith, it was the stuff of nightmares. She was certain she would never have the courage to say a word in such an atmosphere and wondered if others would remark on it. The idea of having an entire flock without any sort of spiritual leader was abhorrent.

She had heard much about the Quakers and their condemnation of life's pleasures as well. Though Judith had more restrictions placed upon her than Louisa-Margaretta, she could still enjoy dancing and cards. Music was what she enjoyed most of all. To think of a group of people depriving themselves of a great deal of culture and society, all because they considered themselves morally superior, angered Judith.

At once, she had the urge to ask Louisa-Margaretta whether she knew more about her cousin's practices. And she realized that she could not.

She shifted in her seat, the hard iron that the old man had praised jostling mightily as they made their way along the road. If she could find one thing that might exonerate Mr Percival Haddington, she realized, she might win back her friend.

That was reason enough to go to the barracks.

$\approx$ 30 $\approx$

It was not dark when they reached the barracks. Manchester was closer than Judith had expected, and with their early start, they arrived in the afternoon. She told her father that they might stop off to surprise their hosts first, but he found a boy whom he paid to mind their trunk so they could go to the prisoner directly.

"I hope the boy is honest." Judith often feared that her father, every bit the mild-mannered clergyman, was apt to be cheated, though it did not happen nearly as often as she might have expected.

Manchester had quite a reputation in Brackenfield. For every story of a poor young man who had gone on to make his fortune, as Louisa-Margaretta's father had, there was one of a man who had died in conditions that were dangerous, dirty, and much more unforgiving than those in the countryside. Judith wondered idly whether the boy would sell everything that she had carefully packed but reflected that she would at least be able to replace it eventually. Some of the people passing them on the street surely did not have the luxury of more than one set of clothes. She had always noticed those of her father's parishioners who could not wear something different on Sundays.

"He will grow restless, yes," her father said, "and he will neglect our things and go off to buy candy. But the guilt, and the promise of a reward, will bring him back."

Judith could not help but laugh. Her father, for all his faults, was not a poor judge of character.

They asked the way to the barracks, and everyone in town knew how to direct them. She only hoped nobody would guess their errand. As indulgent as the likes of the Haddington could be when it came to dueling, it was still illegal, and she knew many shared her father's solemn condemnation of the practice.

When they entered the barracks, they were directed to a colonel who had the unenviable task of overseeing prisoner visits.

"He's not allowed visitors" was their answer. "Once the sentence comes down, they may let him say goodbye."

Judith promised herself that she would not tell her friend Percival's guilt was seen as assured. Surely, Louisa-Margaretta would not wish to know that the army had lost faith in her brother.

"I believe he is allowed spiritual counsel, sir," the rector said.

Judith could already feel herself sweating as she counted the bars in the window, but her father was calm.

"Colonel Chant indicated as much to me. We have traveled a great way in an attempt to carry out his wishes."

Judith's mind worked furiously. She was very nearly sure that Colonel Chant had said no such thing. He was just the sort of man to allow a prisoner no liberties whatsoever. But her father had said "his wishes," and given that Percival

Haddington likely did wish to see him, the sentence was just truthful enough to be a pardonable one—she hoped—in the eyes of the law, if not in the eyes of the Lord.

"Hmm," grunted the colonel. "And you would bring your wife with you? It's no place for a lady."

A hint of a smile played across her father's lips. "I assure you, my wife is always with me."

Judith had to stifle a laugh, and the thought of her father's many half-truths kept her warm in their long, cold march down many passageways. The visiting room held several chairs, even a painting on the wall, and if the room also had bars, at least they were behind curtains.

But all glory in her father's triumph was pushed away by the sight of Percival Haddington. Judith, who knew that he had not been imprisoned long and might face many more nights in a cell, wondered how he could possibly survive such confinement.

His full cheeks, often red from wine, were thin and pale. He moved slowly, and he clutched at her father's hands with his large trembling ones. "You should not have come," he said. "You should not have come."

"I am gratified to be here, my dear." Her father's voice had all the warmth that one might use with a child, though none of the condescension. After that, he did not speak for many more minutes.

Judith was inclined to take the chair nearest the window and pretend to enjoy the view of the yard. Only a glimpse could be seen through a gap in the old curtains.

"This is punishment, I am sure you will say." Mr Percival Haddington's voice rose at the end of his sentence as if he were a child who had been denied his pudding.

"Do you think of it as one?"

He snorted. "My whole life, I knew I would be punished. Though I did not think it would be for something violent."

Mr St Clair nodded. "You did not feel you could follow in the life expected of you. And perhaps you were not suited to it."

Judith did not understand. She looked down at her fingers. She had always been expected to follow the path her parents set out for her, the expectations growing ever higher as she consistently rose to meet them. If someone were to betray her father's faith, it might be Miriam or perhaps even Aaron. But Judith? That was unthinkable.

"I did follow expectations," Mr Haddington said. "All of them, in fact."

"But that is on the outside," her father said. "One's soul is a different matter."

Mr Haddington was ready to unburden himself and seemed to have completely forgotten Judith's presence. "First the army then marriage, nobody could say I did not do my duty."

"And what would your wife say, were she to join us?"

He flushed scarlet. "Her family was awful. They had no regard for her, though they were happy enough to ask for money as soon as the banns were read. She knew everything before she married me, knew that we would never be able to have children, and she chose it."

Mr St Clair fingered his pocket, where Judith knew he kept a small Bible. "With respect, it hardly seems like a choice."

Mr Haddington had no response, perhaps realizing that a young lady of any independent means would hardly be likely to accept a husband with no possibility of children. Ladies in need, on the other hand, entered into such marriages, and worse, with alarming frequency. And they had no doors leading out.

"And how did your wife fare?" Mr St Clair asked. "I cannot pretend that my profession has isolated me from the world, and I am well aware that many people find a balm in matrimony even when a match seemed unsuitable at the outset."

Mr Percival Haddington seemed surprised by the question. "She is well provided for. To own the truth, she seems more troubled by my profession than by my, well, my physical defect." He blushed. "Army life would not always be easy without resources, of course, but I have a small income of my own."

A small income!

Judith twisted in her chair, and only the slight nod from her kind, curious father reminded her not to make her presence felt. But were the monthly sum of Mr Haddington's income given to a poor family for a year, they could keep a dozen children in shoes with meat on the table. Small, indeed. It could only be small compared to the elder Mr Haddington's income. Against all other measures, it was a very healthy sum.

When Mr St Clair did not reply, the prisoner sighed again. "She tells me she is lonely. She longs for a child, but I—we—well, I have no objection if she can find a child. We would raise the babe as our own."

"And this is all you are prepared to offer?"

"It is all I can offer! What else would you have me do?"

"Perhaps take the welfare of this young lady upon your conscience as one of the obligations conferred by your marriage."

They sat in silence for some time. Judith realized that she had never thought Mr Percival Haddington particularly neglectful, despite Tattershall's muted criticism. True, he seemed to prefer wine to his wife's company at dinner, but such could be said for many gentlemen.

However, she had forgotten that even the very wealthy could be measured by the type of expectations her parents had always held. They expected the best and expected to give the best. And she realized that, despite the neglect and unreasonableness demonstrated by what seemed to be nearly everyone in their nation, including the prince of Wales, even the wealthy could count a few examples of happy marriages in their number. Louisa-Margaretta's parents seemed content together, well suited even in their opposite temperaments, but she had to admit that what Tattershall had told her seemed to be true. The only particular in which it did not match Mr Percival Haddington's words was the matter of a child who would not be his. Even then, perhaps his time behind the dirty barracks bars had changed him. Surely, he was thinking more of his wife and his family than he ever had before.

"Does your wife know?" Mr St Clair asked. "Is she aware that you would let a guilty man walk free, perhaps send yourself to the scaffold, because of a childish feeling that you ought to be punished for failing her?"

He shifted. "It is to preserve her as well. Now that she is facing the shame, it is best that everything be seen to quickly so she may make a new life."

"And who will look after her, then, if you are gone?"

Judith blinked, turning fully towards her father. Such a stark question was very unlike him, and his voice held more anger than she could remember hearing in recent years.

Mr Percival Haddington must have felt it, too, for he blanched. "My mother."

"You would abdicate your duty as a husband, the vows you swore before God, and hope that your mother will come to the aid of the woman you have neglected?"

In the following silence, Judith saw her chance. "Is there nothing you could tell us? Nothing, no matter how small, that might help us clear your name?"

He paused then began to speak. And Judith had to keep

from smiling. For at last, she saw a way not only into her friend's good graces but towards a resolution that might clear the whole family's name.

31

Louisa-Margaretta was preparing her trunks. It was intolerable that Judith should go visit Percival when none of his own family had seen him. Her mother wished it, she knew, but Colonel Chant had forbidden her. And her father was part of that prohibition, as was Mrs Peggy Haddington.

"Not that she would go anyway," Louisa-Margaretta murmured to herself, "for she is too occupied with making a spectacle of herself."

Colonel Chant had not thought to say anything about Louisa-Margaretta. Despite the noise she made, the trouble she had always given her parents, and the fact that she must be both the best shot and the finest horsewoman of any lady in the county, she had often been forgotten. As her brothers grew older, they sought professions, married, and had children. Percival was her only brother without children, and she was the only unmarried Haddington. So, all the things that gave her distinction in the schoolroom—her excellent memory, her fine reading voice, and her appetite for naughty tricks—were soon forgotten as her brothers entered the world and she was forced away from it.

But in this one instance, it must work to her advantage. She would call for her horse then go see her brother. It occurred to her, once, that if she were actually to meet Colonel Chant, he might forbid her from speaking with Percival. But she tossed the thought aside as quickly as it came. She would think of something, and she would take money with her. If bribes needed to be paid, she would pay them.

She wondered whether she ought to take more than her purse. Though the threat of highwaymen must be lower in broad daylight than it would be at night, women were still well-advised not to travel alone. Louisa-Margaretta could not think which servant would be willing to go against her parents' orders. It would surely have to be someone young and stupid, and Louisa-Margaretta did not know many of the younger servants by sight. They would be at very great risk of losing their place once it was found out that they were part of such a scheme, but she would intercede with her mother and claim full responsibility.

She walked quickly by her mother's room, where the sound of Mama's weary voice creaking through another prayer made her shudder. She wondered, in anger, how Mr St Clair thought it a decent time to abandon them. For a while, she had avoided reminding herself that her family had given him a living, as she did not like to think of Judith somehow indebted to her. But the thought came into her head constantly. She had heard that he and his daughter had gone to Manchester. Brackenfield was too small a village for that news not to have reached them. But though the rumor included a bit about visiting Percival for spiritual counsel, she did not believe it. Judith would seek forgiveness from her, bring back some wheedling story about how Percival's guilt could be proved and how she never meant her statements as any sort of attack.

Louisa-Margaretta had nearly reached the kitchens when she met Tattershall on the stairs. As usual, her uniform looked perfectly starched, everything down to her shoes without a speck of dust. Not for the first time, Louisa-Margaretta wondered that Tattershall was not a fashionable Parisian maid. There really did seem to be something foreign about the way she carried herself and her manner of speaking. Harriet, for all her admirable effort, never looked half as elegant.

"Wait." She stood still. "I must speak with you."

Tattershall looked surprised but followed Louisa-Margaretta to the unoccupied dining room. It was not only an ideal place for a conversation but a particularly practical one. Louisa-Margaretta began helping herself to food from the sideboard. Nobody else was likely to come down and eat, and it would be wise for her to breakfast well before her journey. Though she had been ready to take all the food she could manage from Cook, it would be less suspicious if she were to eat a large breakfast, as she usually did.

"I was wondering," she said between bites of kidney, "is there someone you might send to accompany me on my ride? Perhaps both a maid and a young boy. We have plenty of horses, and this might be safer."

"Of course," Tattershall said. "Only, perhaps that might be more of a question for Mrs Ridling?"

"No," Louisa-Margaretta said upon hearing their housekeeper's name.

That old gossip would see straight through her and go running to her mother. She had to find another way to get companions out from under her mother's eyes. And if it was too likely to result in discovery, she would risk the road alone. It was unspeakably frustrating, running about the countryside, trying to learn about a stranger. Only the people who had lived and traveled with the dead man could tell her anything about him.

She realized with a start that Tattershall was included in that number. As a wife given special approval to travel with the regiment, Mrs Peggy Haddington might have an inside view, but as her maid, Tattershall would be even better placed to learn everything she could about the gentlemen.

"Did you know anything of Mr Oakley?" she asked.

For the first time, she saw something she could not identify in Tattershall's eyes. It looked like anger. Louisa-Margaretta, who never shied away from strong emotions, was pleased to see it.

"What sort of man was he?" As she watched Tattershall struggle to answer, an idea came to her. "Did he take liberties? Or try to?"

It would explain a great deal, though her mind was quick enough to see the trouble that would create if she were right. If Mr Oakley had been that sort of man and he had tried to take liberties with her sister-in-law, then perhaps Percival—

"No," Tattershall snapped, then she collected herself. "He was—well, never mind that. May he—he was not a bad sort."

She was absolutely stammering. From what Judith had said, even the sight of Tattershall's mistress sprawled on a makeshift fainting couch had not been enough to disturb her before, and yet there she was, very clearly troubled.

Louisa-Margaretta saw her chance. "You know something of him. And if you would tell me, I needn't tell anyone how I learned it. But anything that could help me know him, I could use to clear—" She didn't get a chance to explain her honorable purposes before she was interrupted.

"Miss St Clair," someone announced from the door.

Louisa-Margaretta turned around, her eyes blazing. "Miss St Clair," she fumed. "May I ask the purpose of your visit?"

$$\text{\Large ❧ 32 ❧}$$

Louisa-Margaretta was off, though not before she took a last bite of her breakfast. Judith had always found her friend's appetite both impressive and unladylike.

"Please wait," she said. "I have news for you."

She might not have been able to follow her friend out of the house, had she not already known the way. Louisa-Margaretta could hardly know Wycliff Castle better than Judith did, as it was Judith who took special care to learn all the passageways so she would not find herself in a room where she was not expected or welcomed. Her many days with both Mr Morgan Ramsbury and Louisa-Margaretta had made various corners of the house feel like home to her, but as she nearly ran through the halls, she still felt as if she were in a particularly confusing nightmare.

For Louisa-Margaretta did not wait. She walked towards the stables with a pace so quick that Judith was soon sweating despite the cold. She had no time to feel resentful. She was so busy trying to catch her friend without making it look like she was running.

"Louisa-Margaretta," she managed, "your brother gave me information about Mr Oakley. It may help explain his death."

Louisa-Margaretta stopped, though she still did not look at Judith.

"It has to do with maps." Judith wavered.

She was already failing to explain properly, but her ineptitude at least got Louisa-Margaretta to speak, even if it was only to laugh at her.

"Maps, yes. I'm sure one of Papa's atlases has quite a way with the dueling pistols."

"No," Judith said. "I am not explaining properly. But Mr Oakley has some, and he was not supposed to. He must have stolen them."

Louisa-Margaretta could not help but seem intrigued. "So, Percival thinks this bit about the maps will help him? Even if one could easily purchase a map and Mr Oakley can, at worst, be called a sad little miser?"

Judith's voice faltered. She had seen the point immediately and could not believe that her friend could miss it. "These maps were property of the army. And we're at war."

ical" % 33 %

The two women stood facing each other, Judith insisting that her information was worth something, Louisa-Margaretta refusing to acknowledge or deny it.

"Fine." She stared at Judith as if trying to read the entire conversation in her eyes. "He told you something that may be valuable. Or perhaps not. But you will need to learn more."

Judith could finally breathe again. Though she had been tempted to tell one of Louisa-Margaretta's parents, she was glad that she had gone to her friend. Louisa-Margaretta was the only one person in Brackenfield, after all, would not immediately think Judith's insinuation was mad. At least Louisa-Margaretta admitted that it might be helpful, even if it would not give them everything they needed to clear Percival's name.

"What else do I need to learn?" For a moment, Judith had the mad thought that her schoolroom version of learning would once more be what she needed. That the murderer's name was something she could learn by rote, sitting in a chair, writing one line again and again until it was memorized. That type of learning was what she did well, not trying to pry secrets from people.

The latter, of course, was what Louisa-Margaretta demanded of her. Once again.

"Tattershall was going to tell me something earlier," she said. "I need you to go speak with her and find out what it was."

"Won't you do it?" Judith asked, desperate for a solution that did not involve her talking to the stern maid.

She had a sense that the Haddingtons' servants must look down on her. Over the years, she had heard that certain servants took propriety, and even snobbery, to a height that their employers would find rather amusing. She wondered if Tattershall's coldness to her was of that variety. Judith was not a Haddington, nor was she the sort of friend that Louisa-Margaretta would have made under any other circumstances. Perhaps Tattershall thought the whole friendship an act of charity.

"Servants see things," Louisa-Margaretta insisted. "And she was on the verge of telling me, only she stopped. She'll trust you."

Judith straightened her back, though she still had nothing of her friend's height. It seemed that the Haddingtons were fortunate enough to be tall, like their mother, not short and square like their father. Mr Percival Haddington was rather round in the belly, of course, though that did not seem to be his natural figure. Then again, the thin man Judith had seen weeping in the barracks had hardly looked natural either. It was as if he had lost not only his shape but also his hope.

Judith knew she ought not to refuse any avenue of inquiry that might help the man, and she sighed. "Why do you think she would trust me?"

"Because you're a rector's daughter. You're respectable. Also, she has certainly talked to the families of other rectors in the past. Though that may be out of some sort of defer-ence, she will at least feel like she can have a conversation. With me, she is all efficient politeness."

At one time, Judith would have been offended by the mention of the stark difference between her situation and her friend's. But currently, she thought Louisa-Margaretta might be the loser in the situation. Judith, at least, had three healthy brothers, all happy and well at home. In fact, they were happier than ever since the weather had started to turn. Louisa-Margaretta had one brother who might be condemned to death, and all the others were probably out of their minds with worry. Her mother was mad with prayer, her father with activity, and it seemed that their options for sending someone else to the scaffold were growing fewer by the hour.

"All right," Judith said. "I will do it. But how could I possibly begin to speak with her?"

"Ask her about my riding habit," Louisa-Margaretta said, "the old grey one. Nobody could possibly want to wear that. See if she can alter it to fit you. She'll have to find it and take it in quite a bit."

"Fine," Judith said, unable to suppress a little rumple of annoyance at being asked to wear the riding habit that was good for nobody due to its homeliness.

When she did speak with Tattershall, it was more difficult than she thought. "Miss Haddington asked me to speak with you about her grey riding habit," she began. "She was wondering whether you could alter it for me. Miss Haddington often asks me to ride with her, but nothing fits me."

The woman only nodded. Judith noticed for the first time that she was not particularly old, only severe. Her dark hair, pulled back tightly with no ornamentation, gave her a rather matronly look when paired with her sharp expression. But to see her figure and her skin, she could not be much older than thirty, if that. Judith wondered how she was so experienced, then reflected that she had probably been working since she was a young girl.

Judith had not had such an idle girlhood as Louisa-Margaretta, but beyond learning to cook, she had done very little actual labor. And even the cooking had not been essential, as they could always afford at least a young girl to help in the kitchen. Judith and her siblings had been forced to watch over a hot stove because it was important to Mrs St Clair that her daughters and sons know their way around a kitchen. She'd insisted on teaching her sons, too, though she had not lived long enough to school them all. Judith's aunt Leah, on the other hand, was wary of setting foot in a kitchen after decades of working alongside her sisters, cooking for their large and impoverished family. She had taught Judith and Miriam how to be hostesses, not how to prepare meals.

Judith blinked, tearing her thoughts from her family. "I was wondering if I might try it on now. Perhaps it does not need so much altering after all."

"Yes, miss."

They walked upstairs together. Judith never felt so awkward as when she tried to force someone to confide in her. It seemed that she should have left the task to her friend. All she could think to speak of was riding, which was obviously a pastime she and Tattershall did not share.

"Louisa-Margaretta is so fond of riding," she managed. "Only, I have never been much good at it. We never had horses. But a sorry companion is better than none, as they say. Though in my case, I cannot be sure whether it is true. I certainly slow the horses down, and I slow my friend down a good deal. It is better that I ride and she walk, as we did the other day, for then we are much more evenly matched."

By the time they got to Louisa-Margaretta's room, Judith was nearly sweating with the exertion.

Once she was in the habit itself, though, and the other woman bent near her with her wrist full of pins, Judith finally got a bit out of her.

"Begging your pardon, miss," Tattershall said. "I have a question if you will think it not too forward."

Judith began to breathe. "No, of course not. What is it you wish to ask?"

"Was Mr Percival Haddington well, when you saw him? Only we have all been so worried, and I don't like to trouble my mistress."

Judith nodded. "Has Mrs Peggy Haddington left her bed today?"

"I could not say, miss."

A moment of silence followed. Judith considered her answer. "He is as well as can be expected. He protests his innocence, but I am afraid I have no great faith in the colonel. I have been hoping, each day, for something that might help Mr Haddington. But I know little of him, and I hardly spoke with Mr Oakley. I am afraid I can't say a great deal about either."

Tattershall looked up at her then took out another pin and looked away.

Judith tried to meet her gaze. "Unless there is something you could tell me? Anything."

"I won't have it said that I tell tales." The maid pinned another section of worn grey cloth rather fiercely.

"I'm sure nobody could say such a thing." Judith hoped her voice held understanding, not condescension. "Only, we are all so worried, and it seems that we have learned all we can about that terrible morning."

"Well," Tattershall said. "I know one more thing that

might interest you. But I'll not have my name brought into it, you understand."

"Of course not," Judith said with so much haste that she was sure she did not sound sincere. "There will be no need to mention the source."

Tattershall had finished pinning the habit. She rose, and Judith noticed again how straight she stood.

"There was one in this house," Tattershall said, "who was awake and out of doors very early indeed."

$\maltese$ 34 $\maltese$

The spring sky was darkening by the time Judith reached the village. Even with the hint of twilight, she did not feel safe. If she did not find Mr Haskett soon, she would be forced to give up her task entirely, and she was sure that Mr Percival Haddington's ideas about maps would not be enough to exonerate him. *After all, who else but a guilty man would come up with such an accusation?* If any of their superiors knew of it, they certainly kept it to themselves.

It would not have been proper for her to ask at the inn, not as a young, unmarried woman, and a rector's daughter at that. But she did recognize Harriet's sister, who worked there, and was able to catch her eye as she brought in a delivery at the back entrance.

"If you please," she said. "Are you Miss Sarah Covey?"

The eyes that met hers were suspicious, and Judith hastened to explain herself.

"I am Judith St Clair. I know your sister, Harriet. The two of you are so alike."

She received a smile at that, though a cautious one.

Apparently, all of the Covey sisters were none too eager to converse with strangers.

"Yes, she has spoken of you, Miss St Clair. And I have seen you in church."

Judith nodded hastily. "I have a book that Mr Haskett left behind when he left the Haddingtons'. If he is here, would it be a terrible imposition for you to ask him to come out, just for a moment? I have an errand to run, but I wanted to give it to him first, if I might."

Miss Covey's rather sharp eyes examined her person.

It must be obvious, given the style of Judith's gown, that she had no deep pocket to hide a book, and she tried not to blush at the way such an arrangement must appear. *If only I were arranging some kind of dishonorable tryst with Mr Haskett!* It would be far easier, and far more pleasurable, than asking him whether his recently departed friend was a traitor.

"He's not often here," she said. "He's not one for drinking, Mr Haskett."

"Well." Judith almost left, but she realized that Miss Covey was still standing there.

Even if Mr Haskett was not there often, perhaps he was that evening.

"Do you know where he might be?" Judith asked, growing desperate. Even if it was another place closed to her, she could look for a way to lure him out. Her father would be disappointed to see her returning home so late, but she knew very well that she and Louisa-Margaretta had little time to lose.

"He often walks of an evening," Miss Covey said. "Sometimes, I see him from a distance when I am walking home." The last part was said quickly. Clearly, Miss St Clair was not the only person in the neighborhood worried about the perception of scandal.

"I have never met him walking myself," Judith said. "He must not go near the park, then."

"No, it is at the other side of the village—next to the creek, by the little bridge. It is safe enough there when the water is not high."

Judith wondered at that. She imagined the creek was still fairly high, though she had not had many opportunities to check the last few days. Her brothers, who loved the cold and the mud, could certainly have told her. "Thank you. I will see if he is nearby before I return home."

A noise came from inside, and Miss Covey ducked away without answering.

Hurrying towards the creek through the little village of Brackenfield, Judith saw how the place must appear. She had always felt irritated by the size of the village, the smallest she could have imagined, as well as the bare mountains above it. She longed for the ordinary countryside of her childhood. The inhabitants and visitors who admired the bare and rugged beauty of the peaks made her want to cry as she contradicted them. At first, she had thought Brackenfield a prison, just as Louisa-Margaretta did.

But on that evening, she thought how terrible it must be to be taken away from a place like Brackenfield. Mr Percival Haddington was surely staring at blank walls and bars on a little window—if he was fortunate enough to have a window —as she contemplated the village's rather famous beauty. Surely he wished to feel cold from the exertion of an evening walk rather than a lack of clothing and food. He would be happy enough to return to any home, even a small one, and the large house his parents had bought in a remote area outside Manchester must feel like paradise.

She did not see Mr Haskett at first and wondered if she ought to go home and fetch her father. It was past the hour when she could wander about with any sense of respectability, and Miss Covey must have known that her "errand" was a sham. But if she took her father with her, they might be calling on a parishioner, and she would have a chance to find a warmer garment.

When she looked at the bridge, she saw Mr Haskett. He stared down at the water.

"Mr Haskett," she said, "I am glad to have found you."

He looked up at her, blinking. "I am sorry. Miss St Clair, have you lost your way?"

She gave a nervous laugh. "No, thank you. I know my way quite well. Even on this side of the village, I am hardly far from home."

She looked about. She had thought that when she went to speak with Mr Haskett, many people would be out of doors. Indeed, they were hardly a stone's throw from the nearest homes. But she saw no person very close, though she hoped people would be passing through the village soon. It had not been wise of her to come alone, but Louisa-Margaretta had been summoned to her mama's bedside for prayers, and she could trust nobody else as her companion at that late hour.

He nodded. "Well, then. Good."

"But I had a question for you." Her courage rose.

He still did not move, so she could hardly suppose he intended to shoot her.

When he made no response, she came out with it. "Did you know that your friend Mr Oakley had stolen maps?" At that, she finally got a response.

He straightened, staring at her. "Has that come out, then?"

Her heart rejoiced at the answer, and she realized she had not fully trusted her desires before. If Louisa-Margaretta had accused her of thinking Percival might be to blame, well, it was a just accusation. Judith had thought all along that he was the likeliest murderer, but she suddenly had reason to believe his innocence. If he were the one implicated by the stolen maps, he never would have told her, and Mr Haskett had just confirmed the truth of his tale.

"Yes," she lied. "It seems that they were army maps and he should not have even seen them, much less taken them."

Mr Haskett shook his head. "Well, he had no conscience, and it's no loss to the army. I can say that much. I am not one to say we should not speak ill of the dead."

"Was he selling the maps, then?" Judith knew that officers were expected to have some money of their own, and both Mr Oakley and Mr Green had referred to their paltry pay as a cause of some difficulty, though Mr Haskett had not. He was either able to live rather comfortably or too proud to admit that he needed to find a profession or rank with better remuneration.

"Selling! That might have been something. Then we could have said he was purely mercenary. Like Mr Green, in fact. No, it was worse than that."

Judith was lost. "What has Mr Green to do with it? Was he the one selling maps?"

Mr Haskett shook his head. "I wouldn't be sure that he wasn't. But he has a devilish way of making his living. He cheats at cards, sells anything he can, and never pays his creditors. Just an ordinary man with no money, and if he weren't trying to be a gentleman, I'm sure there would be no trouble about any of it."

Judith contemplated those accusations. "Has he paid his creditors here? One would think that the death of his friend would at least scare him into that degree of honesty."

She remembered Mrs Chomley's sour face in the store as she complained about outsiders who did not pay. Judith had taken it as an insult to her family's honor, whereas the woman was probably thinking of the soldiers.

Mr Haskett laughed bitterly. "It's not this place he has to

worry about. If word gets around of the debts he left in Manchester, our superiors will not look kindly on it. But I doubt he has enough to pay them all. So he just skulks about this place, hoping none of us say anything."

"And none of you have," Judith could not resist adding. "You said that Mr Oakley was worse, and yet, you never spoke ill of him when he was alive."

Mr Haskett shook his head. "I should have. He believed in that Corsican devil. He wanted to help him get here and kill us all off. I'm sure he would not have spared women and children, but Mr Rollo Oakley did not consider the consequences. He only thought about what he saw as glory."

Judith shuddered. Of all the images she had come up with of a French invasion, which many believed to be imminent, that was the most disturbing. Even her father had spoken of how they would survive if they had to go into the mountains with some of his parishioners, local men and women who knew the best places to hide. They were far enough from the coast that they did not have as much to fear as others might, but still, the thought of the French coming after them on their own soil was a chilling one.

"That was why the duel happened." Judith suddenly understood. "The person who found out about his betrayal could not allow it to continue."

"No, they could not," he said, and she gasped.

"It must have been Colonel Chant! For they were heard arguing the night before. And the colonel said something about 'a death with some measure of honor,' which must have meant a death in a duel rather than on the scaffold." Then, with a shiver, she took in the implications of her words. She lowered her voice. "If Colonel Chant committed this murder but is seeing Mr Percival Haddington tried for it, then he has no intention of admitting his guilt. He would kill a guilty man and an innocent one rather than have it said that he harbored a traitor in his regiment."

She trembled. She wanted to be simply angry at the man, but she could not. Instead, terror overtook her. If Colonel Chant was truly so heartless, he might have thought that his plan could eventually be discovered, and yet still, he had not been swayed.

"If that were true," Mr Haskett said, "he would be a dishonorable man indeed. But I cannot allow you to think so ill of him, not when you are so very near the truth."

"Think ill of him?" Judith's laugh sounded a bit mad, even to her. "Why should I not think ill of man who dueled with his own soldier?"

Mr Haskett's face was pale in the dark. "You are wrong. Colonel Chant was not the one who challenged Mr Oakley."

Judith's heart began to slow. "You know who it was, then. Will you tell me?"

35

Judith passed a distracted evening. She wanted nothing more than to share her discovery with Louisa-Margaretta. And she hated to think of what Mr Percival Haddington must be suffering. Her father had often railed against how society was quick to turn its back on the accused, the mad, and the poor. Judith, though their family had been poor enough, had never quite understood the view. After all, when she imagined a prison, she imagined a place where men who had done terrible things might be held so the rest of society was safe in their beds. But with her friend's brother, it was different. Even if he had killed his friend in a duel, it could hardly be supposed that allowing him to sleep in his home would amount to unchaining a murderous lunatic.

She had also supposed places where madmen were sent must be generally helpful, but recently, she had begun to have doubts on that score. Louisa-Margaretta's cousin, a Mr Ephraim Ramsbury, had told her about a lady of his acquaintance who had gone into a madhouse with some disturbance to her spirits and had come out unable to speak. In fact, she hadn't lived many months longer. He was determined that better places ought to be created for the care of such individuals, and though Judith had grown annoyed when he'd gone on about it at length, Louisa-Margaretta's mother had been so moved that she'd offered her services and a sizable sum if he could be involved in the creation of a new system —or at the very least, a new home where young women like the one he had known would not need to risk their lives. Mr Morgan Ramsbury had countered that such a place already existed, only it was more for the use of Quakers. Nobody had asked him much about it after that, and Judith suddenly knew why.

Mr Percival Haddington, she hoped, was only spending an unpleasant night, not risking his life in the sad conditions that she had seen. She prayed it would be the last such night. If she and Louisa-Margaretta could only go to Manchester the next day, they might explain it all. Mr Green was far from innocent, as was Mr Haskett, and finally, they had an explanation for both the challenge and the acts that had provoked it.

Still, she realized that she had fallen far short of a confession. Mr Haskett had still not admitted to murdering his friend. No matter how Judith had pressed him, he would insist that Mr Oakley was already dead when he found the man, and that complicated the story. She had to hope that it would be enough for the army. And she had to find a way of proving the actual culprit, whether it was Mr Haskett or someone else. The coldness in his voice when he described Napoleon had given her a fright. *Was he lying, or was there another murderer?*

Eventually, she gave up on sleep. She contemplated those questions deep into the night before deciding to go downstairs and light a candle so she could read. It seemed a hopeless waste of a candle, but she knew that her father's position as rector had meant that the family could afford such things. They might not be able to have a grand ball with candles glittering on every surface, as one might see at Wycliff Castle, but she could indulge a little sleeplessness.

When she went downstairs, the house seemed so cold, it might have been winter. Only the largest, most vigorous fire could hope to compete with the chill of such a night, and their cold fireplace did not have even the ghost of an ember.

She was walking towards the writing table when she saw a figure in the corner. Her eyes were sufficiently used to the dark for her to see that it was Miriam. But she could make no sense of her sister's clothing.

Miriam was fully dressed, and the chill of the night had plainly entered into her thoughts. She wore Judith's best coat, and the dress she had chosen was more suitable for a walk in the snow than a spring morning. Of course, it was not morning at all.

"Miriam," Judith said, "where are you going?"

She could see the shadow of her sister's face, all moonlit scorn where once sunny adoration had been.

"Away from you," Miriam said.

But Judith waited, knowing that her sister would say more of her plans if her first parry received no reply.

"I am off to Scotland." Her tone softened. "We are to be married."

"We?" Judith asked. "Who?"

36

The sound of the carriage outside was apparent to Judith before Miriam chose to answer. And in that moment, she looked down at the candle she had been carrying—the candle she had hesitated to light, even for one hour, due to a sense of thrift that had been honed over many years of want. She would not shut her eyes to the fact that the family's difficulties could return just as quickly as they had vanished. And neither, she thought, should Miriam. When she spoke, it was no longer in disbelief but in anger.

"Well, the poverty we once knew will be nothing to what you will cause if you go. Father will never see so much of as a day's work as a curate. So I am quite glad you mean to marry for love and forgot the love you once claimed to feel for our family."

She could tell that she had struck her sister, that Miriam had not considered the implications of her rash act. And Judith could by no means guarantee the consequences. An elopement was a grave scandal, to be sure, but it was still a marriage, and though her father would certainly lose his position with the Haddingtons, they might have reason to hope that he would find something else in time.

But she had no time for such niceties as the carriage pulled up and the cold air struck her like a blow. She was outside before her sister. Miriam, despite her professions of love, only stood in the doorway. Judith did not wait but strode right up to the intruder. She found, as she drew near the carriage's occupant, that she could not speak.

"Come in," she heard, followed by the words, "my dear?"

They were tremulous, more like a frail old relative than a lover, and Judith stepped right up to the carriage.

"My sister will not come in," she whispered. Then, much more loudly, she said, "I thank you for delivering the message from my dear friend Louisa-Margaretta. Under the circumstances, you have not an instant to lose in your journey. I hope it is a safe one."

She stepped back, peering at him in the darkness. His clothes were askew, and she sensed that his countenance must betray his discomfort.

"Well then," he said with a little cough. "Miss St Clair, I must beg you—"

"Be off," she said. "For I am sure you wish to make a good journey of it. We have nothing more to say to you, sir."

And she turned towards her home and her sister.

❧ 37 ❧

Judith trembled when she saw her father in the doorway. He had never once given his daughters cause for fear in the past. His quiet disapproval had always been punishment enough, and his disposition was such that he had never resorted to the loud admonishments or gay tongue-waggings of his wife.

And yet, though Judith could not quite make out his expression in the moonlight, she could sense his horror. "It was Miriam who wished to leave, Papa," she whispered, drawing near to him and taking his arm. "I stopped her. And I hope I spoke loudly enough of Louisa-Margaretta's message for any listeners. I will tell the servants that she had some special news for me that could not wait until morning." She spoke quietly, both in fear of some newfound temper of her father's and in what she knew to be a vain hope of keeping the whole sorry business from their servants. A rector's daughter attempting to elope was such a good scandal that Judith had not the slightest hope of its concealment.

Miriam said nothing.

"Miriam," their father said, "is this true?"

Judith felt some triumph as her sister nodded.

"I am sorry," he said.

Judith, shocked, dropped the edges of her shawl, though she still shivered. As the first flush of astonishment wore off, she felt even colder. "Sorry? But, Papa, you need not apologize to me. I simply—"

"I am begging your sister's pardon," he said. "She has been speaking to us for some time, and yet we have not listened."

Judith flushed, though she doubted her listeners could see it. "But, Papa, I have listened! And I—"

"It is my turn to listen now." He held his candle in one hand, taking Miriam's arm with the other. "Come, child, to the library. Judith, you would do well to rest."

She only watched as the two moved away, her father slowly, Miriam stiffly, until she heard the library door close. When she came to, she was shivering harder and sought her bed so she might warm herself enough to think.

38

In the morning, Judith sought her father's counsel, but he looked more tired than she had remembered seeing him.

"It may be too soon for you to speak with your sister," he said. "Perhaps you might call on your friend."

She remembered her last tête-à-tête with Louisa-Margaretta and frowned. Just the evening before, she had wished for nothing more than an opportunity to rush over to Wycliff Castle and share her news. But with her family thrown into chaos, it did not seem important. After all, the Haddingtons should have been looking after their own, rather than leaving all the work to Judith and her father. While they were busy clearing Mr Percival Haddington's name, Miriam had been in much greater trouble than either of them had imagined. They could not keep eyes on two families at once.

"I am not sure I should go, Papa," she said. "They are all at sixes and sevens. They do not know whether to pray or rush off to Manchester or go speak to barristers. I would only be intruding."

He shook his head again. "I'm sure you can find a way to be of use to that family."

"Because I cannot be of use to my own?"

"No," he said, "it is I who have not been of use. Your aunt left, and I neglected all of you."

Judith shook her head fiercely. "You are too hard on yourself."

How could I tell him that, even with more time together, he would still have seen little of what passed in my heart or in Miriam's? Her father simply did not observe those things. She had always considered it an advantage. After Mr Morgan Ramsbury had left, she could hardly eat, and though she only allowed herself to cry in private, her father could see that she was not well. But he never had a sense of the cause. He could see her and her beloved in a room together, each trying and failing not to smile at the other, and miss the point completely.

It was why Judith's mother had always spoken of her directness with her husband. She said she could not be coy and romantic, for if she did not speak plainly of her own regard for Mr St Clair, he would misunderstand her meaning. "If I had waited for him to notice that I esteemed him highly, we would never have married. So, let that be a lesson to you, my dears. Even very wise men can be blind in certain areas. You had best make your feelings as plain as your manners will allow."

When Judith thought back, she knew little of her parents' courtship. She remembered that her mother had traveled around the country a great deal, and when her parents married, Mama had newly arrived in London from Manchester. Other than that, their father's lack of observation was the only piece of the story she had been given.

It may well end up being a much more romantic courtship than will ever take place within the family in the future, Judith reflected. The one man she loved, she could not possibly marry. And Miriam had dishonored herself more with her attempted elopement than Judith would ever have believed. If she wanted any degree of respectability, she would need to get as far away from the gossip as possible and marry quickly.

And though Miriam was less spoiled than Louisa-Margaretta, Judith thought that she would hate the idea just as much. Louisa-Margaretta had consented to stay in Brackenfield, but she certainly had not married. And it looked as if she was determined to remain as she was.

As Judith walked down the chilly path to Wycliff Castle, after her father had all but pushed her out the door, she reflected that at least she had the comfort of friendship in her spinsterhood. She might be a poor spinster, and Louisa-Margaretta a rich one, but it was better that they had some companionship in their respective situations.

39

"Oh, Judith," Louisa-Margaretta said. "It is hardly a love story, but I have decided whom I shall marry. So, perhaps you can come in and talk to me. I am sure you know little of trousseaus, but I must speak to someone about the preparations, and all the women in this house are half mad or fully mad at present."

Judith glared at her friend. Marriage, as it happened, was the last thing she wanted to speak of. It seemed cruel that at the very moment Miriam's reputation might well be crumbling, Louisa-Margaretta had decided to accept a suitor. And when her brother might be about to die. It was selfish and unfeeling, even for a person who had a lifetime's experience in thinking only of her own comfort.

"I must go to my family," Judith said, her words clipped. "But I spoke to one of the soldiers yesterday, and I have information that I must share."

Louisa-Margaretta's smile was still broad. "Ah, spoke to a soldier, did you? Well, they do love to speak with lovely young ladies. Perhaps that is why they are still in Brackenfield."

Judith thought of leaving. She did not have to tell Louisa-

Margaretta anything, after all. But she realized that if she left in a fit of ill humor, even the princess of the Haddington family would know something was amiss. Under normal circumstances, Judith's morality would never allow her to keep such a piece of information. Though she struggled, she knew that it would be a sin to let Mr Percival Haddington suffer just because his sister was a trying young woman. And perhaps, thinking of Louisa-Margaretta going on about her trousseau, taking joy in her upcoming nuptials while hardly noticing that her friend was pale with sorrow, "trying" was not quite the word Judith would choose.

"First, the news about your brother." Judith willed herself not to cry. As much as she wished to be useful to Miriam, she could not simply leave because she was angry. She would have to share what she had learned. "Mr Haskett was the one who asked for the duel. I believe that his love for the rules of the army was not enough to counter his disgust that Mr Oakley would give secrets to the French. To make it worse, it seems as though Mr Oakley was not selling them at all. He was truly a turncoat."

Louisa-Margaretta nodded. "So it was Mr Haskett all along. People with that level of love for order are seldom safe. They would kill a man for less. Mr Haskett is the sort of man who believes we should cut off the hand of a thief, no matter how impractical a solution it is for all parties."

Judith hesitated. "He claims that he did not kill Mr Oakley. But he will admit that your brother knew nothing of the duel. When Mr Haskett arrived there, the body was not yet cold. Someone must have been there just before him, and if we have any evidence of where your brother was in the early morning, that will help the army know for certain that he is innocent."

Louisa-Margaretta looked at her coldly. "You believe him to be innocent, then?"

Judith's eyes flashed. "I have spent the better part of my days and devoted every waking hour to proving it. And what I have learned from Mr Haskett, and from your brother himself, is what we will use to convince the rest of the world."

For a moment, she hoped that the news of the duel would overtake any other news in Brackenfield. For as much as she had wanted Louisa-Margaretta's counsel in the matter of Miriam's engagement, she began to realize that it was not safe. If she must lie, it would have to be to the whole village.

"Well," Louisa-Margaretta said, "why do you speak of your family needing you? Surely nobody is ill. We must go to Manchester if Mr Haskett will not go himself. We must leave today."

Judith shook her head. Her voice trembled. "Perhaps you can send your father. And I must tell you more news about the army men in Manchester."

Louisa-Margaretta was already looking for something to wear for a long journey. She seemed determined, but she did not have the flush and look of joy that Judith had been taught to expect from new brides, or even from young women in love. She herself had worn that look before she'd learned the truth about Mr Ramsbury. Louisa-Margaretta looked as if she were nearly dizzy with excitement, but she had ceased talking of marriage as soon as she received news of Mr Haskett.

"Well, tell me, then," she said, her back to Judith. "I can have my father take me. Then I can relay the information, and he will make sure we are seen quickly."

"Mr Green left," Judith said. "He had debts, here and in Manchester, that he could not pay. And he must have worried that suspicion would fall on him after Mr Haskett said he would come forward. Mr Green said he did not know who the guilty party was but that he feared for his life."

Louisa-Margaretta turned to stare. "Mr Green? He cannot have left."

Judith's stomach turned. She could not remember the last time she had eaten. And many days of eating poorly were beginning to make her feel even weaker in her grief. "I have it on good authority that he did."

She turned to leave, but Louisa-Margaretta grabbed her arm.

"But he—no, not Mr Green. No. Whose authority?" Louisa-Margaretta's words broke before she could get them out. Her eyes were wide, and she held Judith's arm too tightly.

"I saw him leave," Judith snapped. She had still not thought the story through. It would be preposterous, Mr Green happening to stop by her home in the middle of the night, when the roads were not safe and nobody but a highwayman would set off on a journey. And since the story about his delivering an urgent message from Louisa-Margaretta was a lie, Judith would be muddying it if she told a different lie. But it was too late to think of that.

"He told me, before he left," she managed. "Because we were asking questions, I believe he wanted me to hear his story of innocence." She paused, nearly holding her breath.

If Louisa-Margaretta did not believe her, she was certain to fish out the whole story. Usually, when she sensed a lie, she was relentless. "And how did he seem to you?"

Judith had not expected the question. "Well, sad, I suppose. And scared." It was rather vague, but it would have to do.

"Why would Mr Green tell you and not someone in my family?" Louisa-Margaretta asked.

"Perhaps he realized you would be angry." Judith's voice faltered. "I was not happy with his words, but I wouldn't stop him from leaving."

"Well, you ought to have stopped him," Louisa-Margaretta said.

"Why?" Judith asked. "And how? He had a carriage with horses and a driver, and I had only my wits."

She had allowed herself to grow angry. With every moment she was kept from Miriam, she grew more furious at Louisa-Margaretta for being unable to see past her own elegant family's troubles. Judith knew that if she were asked about a trousseau again, she would be in very great danger of telling the truth, simply to illustrate the point that other families in the world besides the Haddingtons had troubles.

"He was to stay here until we were married." Louisa-Margaretta started to cry. "Oh, hell and damnation, he must have murdered Mr Oakley himself!"

❧ 40 ❧

ouisa-Margaretta saw her friend soften. Judith had
been angry and withdrawn all morning. She was
usually the first to comfort Louisa-Margaretta, but
she looked as though she wished for a set of dueling pistols all
her own. Still, Louisa-Margaretta's tears were rare, and Judith
was not impervious to them.

"You should leave," Louisa-Margaretta managed. "You
have done enough."

"I'm sorry," Judith said. "I did not think that he was to
blame, and I thought that as long as we could clear your
brother, perhaps—"

"Leave now," she demanded. "Leave me."

As soon as Judith departed the room, her tears were much
greater. She cried as she had hardly cried since girlhood. Even
when she was separated from her beloved, a sense of love and
justice in her heart had made the tears almost sweet. Nothing
was sweet anymore. It was all bitterness.

Louisa-Margaretta's room was large, and she ran to one of
the windows. She wished she could escape, but she could not
have anyone find her like that. She was already afraid that

anyone who saw her would see a wreck of a young woman who had once been brilliant and proud.

She had nearly accepted Mr Green. In fact, she would have accepted him as soon as they'd had a chance to speak. It seemed that her family situation was so hopeless, she had forgotten how to cope on her own, and she thought that a weak and cowardly man would be her best hope of salvation.

He had said that he wished to admire her from afar, and like a young fool, she had believed him. Instead, he had shown no qualms about abandoning her. She had been on the verge of marrying a man who, in addition to being far below her station, had no regard for her family's troubles. Mr Green, for all his talk of love, thought only of himself.

She cried so long, she hardly knew the reason, and eventually, she realized that she was crying for Isaac, her beloved. Ever since he had failed to respond to her letters, she had been thinking up reasons. Perhaps both her letters had gone astray. Perhaps he had enlisted in the army and was even then in France, or perhaps he had left for some distant colony. But when she confessed to Judith that he did not love her, that explanation had felt the truest, and she was beginning to accept it.

For months, she had made the best of things in Brackenfield. She had a friend beside her, and she had the knowledge that she was loved by a most worthy gentleman. In addition to all that, she had every sort of indoor and outdoor pursuit to amuse her. But it had been an empty promise, her peaceful country life, and she was realizing it. She had allowed her parents to decide everything for her. She had ceased to have the slightest influence in the direction of her own life.

Tattershall knocked at the door, and Louisa-Margaretta tried to hush her sobs for a moment, though she did not allow her to enter.

"Do not come in. What is it?"

"I brought you a tray."

"Leave it outside the door. I do not require it yet."

She had fallen onto the bed, where she had been crying, and she had an image of herself. She was a young lady of means, still beautiful and intelligent, who allowed herself to spend half the afternoon crying in a large, warm bed. All the enterprise she had used to clear her brother's name would be wasted if she kept to her room and accepted her meals on trays. She would be little better than Peggy, refusing to speak, or Mama, refusing everything except the empty promise of prayer.

With a start, she stopped her tears, sitting up. She had the blessing of a good stomach, and she knew she could not afford to go without food. She waited until Tattershall's footsteps grew faint, which seemed to take some time. Vaguely, she wondered why Tattershall bothered with her if Peggy was still indisposed. Surely the young Mrs Haddington required all her attention, and Harriet should have brought the tray.

When Louisa-Margaretta brought it into her room, she sneered in disgust. It held a piece of toast and one small egg, along with some tea and a very small cup of broth—very lady-like, and not nearly enough for Louisa-Margaretta. She would go down to breakfast and load her plate properly. She considered drinking the broth, but it smelled funny to her. Probably it was another of Mama's Lenten fancies, broth so weak it was worse than water. She knew that a regular breakfast would set her up.

After cleaning her face and doing everything she could to make herself presentable, she joined her father for breakfast. "Papa," she said, "we are off to Manchester today."

❧ 41 ❧

On Easter morning, Judith rose early.

She had been sleeping poorly, and waking early was part of it. In those fitful hours, she might have gone to speak with Miriam. She had tried many times over.

Miriam, she saw, was not in good spirits, though she spoke often enough with their father. During the daytime hours, she took what had formerly been Judith's place at the piano. It was as if picking out tunes, each one more intricate than the last, was the only thing that soothed her. And she did little else.

Judith tried to raise the topic with their father. "She will go mad if she speaks to no one."

"Her spirit is in a difficult season, my dear," he told her. "If we try to bring on the spring too soon, we will only hurt dear Miriam. Let her play if she wishes it."

On Easter morning, Miriam was already awake, sitting at the instrument. It was too early to play without waking her brothers, so she had music before her, and she touched the keys without letting them sink.

Judith, who had always considered herself rather a master

of J.S. Bach's compositions, felt a pang of jealousy. *How long has it been since I sat down and played for hours?* She had been too occupied with Louisa-Margaretta's troubles. And yet, she knew nothing of the Haddingtons.

She heard plenty of talk in the village, of course. How young Miss Haddington had gone off to Manchester with her father, and they had brought Percival back with them. He had resigned his place in the army, but the Haddingtons had seen him formally cleared of all charges. The general consensus was that the handsome and quiet Mr Green had killed his friend then bribed a ne'er-do-well groomsman to drive him away in a stolen carriage for a great deal of money. The carriage itself had been recovered, but the groomsman and Mr Green remained at large.

"Miriam," Judith said, "happy Easter."

Miriam only shook her head. "Not a happy one. But I suppose it is Easter now."

Judith suppressed a sigh. The day on which their savior had sacrificed his life in an almost theatrically grotesque fashion really ought not to be a day when being crossed in love was considered a tragedy. Judith herself, after all, had managed to survive after Mr Morgan Ramsbury had given his horrible revelations. And if she still thought of him rather constantly, she managed to do something useful with herself besides sigh over Bach. In fact, she was about to help prepare the family's breakfast, as she did every morning, and she did not think that helping would be beyond Miriam.

The words came out before she could stop them. "Miriam, would you help me set the table, or are such tasks beyond you?"

The sadness on her sister's face would have made another young woman weep. "Nothing is beyond me, Judith. But thank you for your concern."

Judith sat on the bench awkwardly, close enough that she

could have played the lower lines of Bach. "I am concerned. But I cannot stand to see you like this. Making yourself useful will help heal this wound."

"What would you know of heartbreak?" Miriam asked. "You cannot possibly know what will help me."

When Judith was silent, Miriam gave a funny little laugh. "Oh yes, your suitor. Mr Morgan Ramsbury. But just because you capriciously rejected him does not mean you know what it is to be betrayed. He was a perfect gentleman, and he would have married you, as I'm sure you are aware."

That stung. Judith had supposed herself protected by her discretion. But she knew that to everyone but her father, it must have been obvious. She had spent long days at the Haddingtons, even when Louisa-Margaretta was otherwise occupied, and she knew how much joy had infused her soul during that time. It would have been impossible for Miriam to miss, though she supposed her sister might not know the full details of Mr Ramsbury's strange religious leanings.

"I am trying to keep myself occupied for the good of our family, Miriam," she said, "and you might do the same."

Miriam shook her head. "You stay within the family circle because you fear to go elsewhere. Papa is calling Aunt Leah back, you know, to care for me. Then where shall you go? If you're going to reject men like Mr Ramsbury, you may as well leave off thinking of society entirely. Get thee to a nunnery."

Judith was puzzled. Miriam knew the history of their country, and of their church, as well as Judith did.

Judith chose to speak only of the literal meaning of her words. "You know we do not have nunneries, Miriam." She tried again to keep her voice light, rather than feeling the bite of the words.

"Well then," Miriam said. "Do leave me. Whether you find a nunnery or not."

"Miriam." Judith reached for her sister's hand.

"No," Miriam said. "I will thank you for keeping me from Mr Green. I believe that I will spend each day realizing just how unworthy he was. But now I will thank you for leaving."

Judith nearly ran to the kitchen, where she tried to hide her tears as she and Sarah prepared breakfast. It was hardly light out and much too early, but every rector's family had to get breakfast ready on such days as Easter. They all needed to get dressed and go to church as quickly as they could to help with preparations. Though her father was not like the sad Mr Lewis, given to chastising his parishioners whenever they did come if he decided their attendance was not in keeping with his requirements, the church was sure to be full. Her father did not hold with the custom for punishing those parishioners who had not attended church, or paid their tithes, each Easter. Rather, during the season, he took special care with his visits. In that way, each family that had not demonstrated in full its commitment to the church would have a chance to rectify it. He could always report to the bishop that thus-and-such matron had resolved to attend more often or that so-and-so's family had made a considerable contribution without it being thought that his care was more for his flock's well-being than for the health of the church's coffers.

That did not stop Judith from repenting. Easter had always been a day of guilt for her. When she reflected on the sacrifice that the day would be spent on, her endeavors seemed insignificant by comparison. In the past year, she had lost her mother and done some things to ensure the health and safety of Miriam and their brothers. *But to what end?*

Her brothers would likely have done well in Brackenfield without her. They already had new friends, new amusements, and mountains that they delighted in climbing. Miriam, in contrast, seemed to have been erased by their mother's death and the subsequent changes to their lives. Perhaps she wanted to leave Brackenfield just as badly as Judith and Louisa-

Margaretta did. But Judith had never taken the time to speak with Miriam about her wishes for the future. Judith reflected, sadly, that she was perhaps more guilty even than Louisa-Margaretta in terms of selfishness. For at first, she had wanted all the time she could steal with her beloved. And after, she had wanted only to speak of her heartbreak, not to listen to any complaints of her sister's. Louisa-Margaretta, having been spoiled all her life, could hardly help ignoring others' desires. Judith, her superior in temperament and sense of duty, ought to have known better.

By the time Judith had set out breakfast and eaten a very small meal with her father, the day grew lighter. Her brothers tumbled downstairs, but she left them to Miriam. With the sting of her sister's words so fresh in her mind, she could not stand to be in the same house a moment longer. Because she could not cry, the unshed tears seemed to collect in her heart, where they weighed heavily.

In the church, she felt some calm as she lay out her father's vestments. She had been helping him prepare them for a week and wanted to make sure her little repairs and adjustments would hold. It was his first Easter in that parish, after all, and she felt some pride seeing the fine surplice. Though he was not the same height as the previous rector, who had also been much stouter of build, he would look well in it. He liked to use another for weddings and christenings, but she thought the Easter one the most beautiful. And his clear blue eyes were set off by the bright white linen—she could tell. She had always envied that, though her mother had told her that her own hazel eyes were just as beautiful.

"Thank you, my dear," her father said.

As he turned to go into the sanctuary, she realized she had not buttoned the very top of the surplice and frowned.

"I'm sorry, father," she said. "I was distracted. I should have remembered from last year."

"How were you to remember?" He chuckled a bit. "Even your mother, who helped me with these garments for decades, never quite got it right. It is different when you set them out for another. For me, it is something I do not think of, and therefore, I do it the right way, relying only on the memory of my hands."

"Did Mama really get it wrong?" she asked. "But wouldn't she have known it well?"

"The easiest way to remember," her father said, "is to put them on and wear them the whole day. Trust me, my dear. If I were to try and wear your things, I am sure there would also be some reversal."

"But you would not make this mistake with your own. And surely no curate or vicar with any experience would forget the top button," she mused.

"No, my dear. I suppose not."

"Father," she said breathlessly, "I must leave. I will be back for the service if I can be."

He stood, waiting for her explanation, but she only pressed his hands. "It is about Louisa-Margaretta. I am so sorry. I will bring her if I can."

And she was out the church and down the road to Wycliff Castle before he could ask her for an explanation.

42

Mr Oakley's sash was tied at the right. It was supposed to be tied at his left, but it was tied at the right. That thought kept Judith running along the path, much faster than her legs would normally have carried her. After weeks of complaining about the cold in the mountains of Brackenfield, she was warm in what felt like moments. The size of the Haddingtons' home seemed cruel, as she could see it nearly the whole walk, and yet it seemed to take her hours to reach the door. *Oh, for a horse!* After breaking with Louisa-Margaretta and not eating well, then losing many hours of sleep over Miriam, Judith realized how weak her constitution had become. She ought not to have allowed herself to falter. She needed a great deal of strength, but she had none.

By the time she reached the house, she tried to spend a moment composing herself before asking for an interview. But her arrival had been noted, and the large door swung open much more quickly than she would have preferred.

As an intimate friend of Louisa-Margaretta's, the only young lady in the county with such a claim, she was used to being welcomed into the home well before guests were generally expected. Not all family members might be dressed, but she could still say that she wished to be shown to her friend without exciting any suspicion.

On that day, she asked to be shown to the murderer's room first.

The room was dark. Though the day looked to be cloudy, it was not so early that some dawn light couldn't brightened things. But the individual preferred to rest in darkness.

Judith tried to steady her nerves. She had already been announced, and she had made no secret of where she was going. It was not some little dueling ground with nobody about. If she were to lose her life in that bedchamber, it would be well-known.

"Good morning," she managed. She received no greeting back, and yet she did not think the bed's occupant was asleep. "I wished to speak with you. About Mr Oakley."

After she said it, she heard the woman stir.

"Mr Oakley," the woman said. "I should have known we would be found out, eventually. And all this for nothing. It is rather a waste."

Judith moved closer to the bed but could not bring herself to draw back the bedcovers. She knew that she should simply leave, allow the confession to stand as it was, but her horror and sadness kept her rooted to the spot. There she had been, thinking that more age and experience in the world would improve her life, and yet, in that woman's case, it seemed to have only caused destruction.

"Why?" Judith asked. "Why throw away your life and his?"

A mumbled answer followed, and Judith waited. When she heard the reason clearly, she left. She wondered whether she ought to say anything. Perhaps Mr Oakley's death ought to remain unexplained. *If the military could not find a culprit, and the magistrate had not taken it upon himself to interfere where the army had fallen short, then what would be the harm in allowing a mystery to go on?*

She hated the idea. Mr Oakley, it seemed, had not been a good man. He was certainly a spy, and he had dragged others into his schemes without thinking of their well-being. But he had not deserved to die, certainly not at the hands of someone who had attempted to deceive him. Judith, who shared her father's distaste for even the lauded killing on the battlefields, could not allow such a thing to pass.

She could not, however, bear the burden on her own. She needed to find Louisa-Margaretta.

43

She found Louisa-Margaretta in the music room. Judith found it very strange how most of the rooms in Wycliff Castle went unused. Even when they had guests, the parties tended to use only a small set of them. And the music room had always been a favourite. Her friend sat by a little table next to the harp and pianoforte, a quill and an inkwell in front of her.

"What are you doing?" Judith asked.

It was not a desk, and if Louisa-Margaretta were to spill any of the ink on the beautiful sofa, the mistake would be a costly one. Though, of course, the Haddingtons had more places where guests and family members could sit than nearly any family in England.

Louisa-Margaretta's eyes narrowed. "Trying to write my own music since you will not help me."

Judith started. She had completely forgotten about the music scheme and wondered how quickly her friend had decided that she could do all of it alone. Judith had thought she did have some gift for composition, though she was absolutely useless when it came to putting words to her musical ideas.

"And how do you get on?"

Louisa-Margaretta threw down her quill. It happened to be on the album where she had been trying to write, so it only left a splatter across the clean white paper, but Judith could see she would have been just as indifferent if had left horrid black stains on the furniture.

"I do not get on at all, thank you very much for your concern. I asked you to write the music, and if you had only done so, I wouldn't have wasted days trying to do it on my own."

"Perhaps I could still help with it," Judith said. "My sister seems to think I require an occupation."

Louisa-Margaretta did not laugh but sank down behind the harp. "I am sure that you did not come here to speak to me about music. Why are you not preparing for Easter?"

At last, Judith found her footing. She knew Louisa-Margaretta took pride in their shared application of intellect and daring, so she presented her solution. "I discovered something about what the soldiers told us. The person who put on Mr Oakley's sash could not have been a soldier. A soldier would never have put it on the wrong side. So that means, not only that your brother is innocent but that we cannot blame Colonel Chant, Mr Haskett, or Mr Green."

Louisa-Margaretta picked out a few notes on the harp, but Judith could tell her indifference was feigned. She was curious, though she tried to hide her feelings behind the familiar strains of "Jesus Christ Has Risen Today" that Mrs Haddington had doubtless been requesting daily as Easter approached.

"I am sure we can blame them for a great many things," Louisa-Margaretta said. "Especially Mr Green."

Judith looked up sharply at that, wondering if her friend

had guessed, but her heart eased a bit as Louisa-Margaretta went on.

"And of course, even if it was not a soldier, that is hardly a solution. Who else would have both known about the duel and gone out to kill Mr Oakley at that time?"

"Someone who very nearly knew how soldiers were supposed to dress," Judith said. "Perhaps the wife of a soldier."

Louisa-Margaretta narrowed her eyes. She was not stupid, and she knew well that Judith could be considering only one such person. "I will not have you dragging Peggy's name into all this. You were wrong to accuse Percival, and you are wrong to accuse his wife. She still keeps to her bed. How could she have killed a man? I can tell you that she is useless, anyway. If anything, I am the only person who is not a soldier and who can shoot. And I'm sure you will not try to tell the army that I am guilty of a murder. Or perhaps you will."

In fact, in that moment, Judith could easily see how someone might believe Louisa-Margaretta guilty of murder. Her friend had both the wits and the energy for such a task, and she was currently plucking at the harp strings with such anger that she seemed easily capable of violence. But Judith knew Louisa-Margaretta never saw the necessity of hiding her feelings. If she had despised Mr Oakley, she would have said so quite openly.

"The person who shot killed him would not have to be a good shot," Judith said, "if he did not expect to duel."

"Well, he went to the place where he was killed with dueling pistols in the early morning, so I can hardly think of what else he may have expected."

"But if he met someone there first. Someone he trusted, perhaps a woman."

"That is a scandalous idea indeed! How could you suggest something like that about my sister-in-law?"

"She was desperate for a child, and Mr Oakley had promised to help her in exchange for all the information about the army she could procure."

That was the first information to shock Louisa-Margaretta. Her eyes widened.

Neither she nor Judith were quite so naive as to believe that married men and women never broke the strictures placed upon them, but even the unhappy Mrs Peggy Haddington had seemed to love her husband, and she certainly did not have a wealthy, powerful, or even loving family who would have protected her if she were to fall victim to public scandal.

Louisa-Margaretta cleared her throat. "Even if that were true, which I am sure it cannot be, what more information could she gain? Percival was Mr Oakley's equal."

"Yes, and they were both taken quite seriously as soldiers. If a soldier's wife is not quite in the right place, or if her reticule is unusually heavy, she will not easily be suspected— especially if she can pretend to be stupid. Your sister-in-law told me she excelled that that."

"Well," Louisa-Margaretta said, "I can't pretend to approve of that arrangement, but it seems at least to have been an amiable one for both parties. If my sister-in-law has not, in fact, gotten a child out of it, why would she wish to end it in a murder? Surely there is no sense in that."

Judith bit her lip. She had not, in fact, thought to ask that question. As soon as Mrs Peggy Haddington had confessed that she wanted Mr Oakley to "give her a child" in exchange for her help with the theft of army documents, she had been overcome by embarrassment and sadness. But that did not explain why Mr Oakley had been killed. Perhaps he had decided that he wouldn't keep his end of the bargain after all. Though Judith remembered what she had heard about Mr Oakley coming to visit when his friend and fellow officer, Mr

Percival Haddington, had been otherwise engaged. She had forgotten and never managed to ask Harriet what exactly she meant, but surely, it had referred to some kind of liaison. She had heard the uncertainty in Harriet's voice, the sense that she was telling tales about rather dark secrets.

"Mr Oakley had been discovered," Judith said. "Mr Haskett intended to expose his conduct. And I imagine Mr Haskett made some plan for that, even if he himself were to be killed in the duel. He would not have allowed this betrayal to remain undiscovered."

"So, dear Peggy went out first and shot Mr Oakley so he would not expose her as an adulteress? It is preposterous. I mean, consider the child. Even if his natural parent had been Mr Oakley, legally, his father would have been Percival, and few would have said more about it. It takes a very odd-looking changeling for tongues to wag, and even then, they would have said that the babe looked just like somebody's funny old Auntie Martha."

Judith, who had always looked like a bit of a changeling in her own family, sighed. It was a flimsy reason for a murder, to be sure. But then, Mrs Peggy Haddington seemed to have lost her wits even before the murder, and she was certainly without them currently. Perhaps, for her, rage and passion were reasons enough.

"I must go speak with her again," she said. "You will not go with me?"

"Absolutely not," Louisa-Margaretta said. "You have done quite enough, Judith, in terms of accusing every member of my family of the most scandalous involvement with this murder. Do you have no sense of the shame you cause?"

Judith nearly told her friend everything about Miriam's elopement. If only she understood that Judith was trying to bring justice, not throw stones at her friend's family. "I never meant to cause you shame, Louisa-Margaretta."

"Well, you have done it all the same. Just because you use delicate words does not mean I will excuse the betrayal behind your behavior."

"Louisa-Margaretta," Judith began, "in trying to solve this murder, am I not trying to spare your family shame?"

The young lady did not answer, only stood, which was a clear dismissal. "I am going to prepare my Easter bonnet and make sure it looks well with my gown," Louisa-Margaretta said. "If you have any sense, you will walk to the church with our family before your father sends someone to retrieve you."

❧ 44 ❧

Judith approached the sleeping woman softly, sitting on the edge of her bed. Tattershall stood in the corner, doing something with the various tinctures that the young Mrs Haddington was supposed to take. As far as Judith could tell, none of them had helped poor Peggy's spirits or her sleep in the least. She looked as pale as a ghost, and from her breathing, it seemed that she did not truly sleep. Perhaps she simply did not want to open her eyes and see the world that faced her.

"Mrs Haddington," Judith said, then "Peggy" when she received no response. "How did you kill Mr Oakley?"

At last, something. The woman rose and shook her head. "I did not kill him."

Judith frowned. Earlier, Peggy had been quite clear that she'd had an arrangement with Mr Oakley, one that had fallen through—an arrangement that was to end in the birth of a child.

"I wondered if perhaps you loved him, or he you," Judith said. "They say that passion can make a person mad."

She did not believe it, not really. At the height of her

heartbreak, she might have walked out in the early morning to cry, insensible of the cold, but she would not have taken a dueling pistol with her. Even Louisa-Margaretta had never shown violent tendencies when she had talked about the unsuitable man in her past, though of late, she had become almost violently bitter. Apparently, though, others felt differently.

"Mr Oakley did not love me," Mrs Haddington said softly. "Of course not. Unlike Percival, he truly loved his wife." She sank into the pillows again.

Judith touched the woman's hand, trying to bring her back to the room, to the conversation. "Wife? But Mr Oakley had no wife."

In the corner of the room, Tattershall went very still. Then she ran.

45

Judith fell behind almost immediately. Tattershall was quicker than she was and more desperate. But only so many doors led out of the house, and Judith guessed that Tattershall would leave by the back door, not the front. When Tattershall reached the woods, the folds of her skirt caught on a tree, and that gave Judith the moment she needed to catch up.

By the time the maid had torn herself free, she turned to face Judith, defiance and hatred in her face. "Don't come one step closer. I killed him, and I could kill you."

Judith needed no more threats. She stood rooted to the spot. "Why did you kill him?" She could not help asking, though her voice had all but deserted her. "Mrs Haddington said that he loved you."

Tattershall coughed. "He loved me, and the cause. That is, at first. Then, when we were finally making progress, he lost his nerve over a few maps—said he wanted to give it all up and I should cooperate. He worried that I might be with child."

Judith tried to breathe. "A child that you would have giv

to Mrs Peggy Haddington in exchange for her help with the maps."

It was not quite as scandalous as she'd feared. Instead of becoming an adulteress, poor Peggy had hoped simply to become a mother by accepting a babe from a married couple.

Tattershall, or rather Mrs Oakley, laughed wildly. "She believed that story for months. And I didn't mind the visits from my husband. But I would not have allowed a child to interfere with our plans. And there never needed to be any result, just the hope. That was enough to keep the stupid woman quiet."

At last, Judith began to feel threads of anger gathering through her fear. "You will pay for it now. You will be imprisoned for what you did."

"You won't capture me," Tattershall said. "And you have no proof that I killed my husband, so suspicion will stay on your friend and her precious family, as it should."

That had also occurred to Judith. But she knew that the wild woman before her harbored all the keys to her own destruction, if only she could be tricked into giving at least one of them away.

"I'm not sure that you were ever married." Judith knew she still had only the strange woman's word about everything that had taken place. "Perhaps you only fancied yourself his wife."

It worked. Tattershall, or Mrs Oakley as she ought to have been called, let out a cry of physical pain. "Ignorant girl! There is a record of our marriage. It took place in Manchester, on January 17, 1811. It is just as legitimate as the marriage of your own parents, if not more so."

Judith gasped. She had never heard her mother's memory invoked with such anger, and the venom in it took her momentarily by surprise. But she could not be truly offended, because anyone who would make such a comment could have no sense of how respectable and loving her parents were. She reflected, as her heartbeat quickened, that the woman must see demons and calculation in every marriage. Judith only had to keep her speaking. She could not be sure whether Tattershall hid a pistol in the folds of her uniform, and apparently, the maid was a rather good shot.

"And Mr Green? Did you send him away?"

She smiled. "Yes, I knew the fool would run the first chance he got. I wrote him letters anonymously, which was rather perfect. He never thought to compare them against my handwriting, though he tried to match them to everyone who lived in this house. Since I was the only person who had been near his things, it was as if nobody had gone near them. My presence goes unnoticed, unremarked. He knew someone was close, and this made him fear for his life. I thought either your friend or your sister would go with him, which would have added a great deal to the distraction, but neither was quite that silly."

Judith's face burned. "Neither of them is silly at all. Louisa-Margaretta is adventurous, and Miriam has a kind heart. Mr Green, if he sought to trespass on those good qualities, did wrong by both of them."

Tattershall took a step forward, and Judith stepped back. She could not hold her ground, and she saw no reason to try. *What on earth will I do if this woman keeps running?* She could not chase her all the way up a peak. Judith, faint from hunger and in great want of exercise, would collapse.

"Neither of them silly, really? Your friend Louisa-Margaretta has been running all over the countryside, and still, she never managed to find the woman who saw that her skirts were mended and clean. Harriet is useless, and my work has tripled since I came to this house. I shall be glad to leave it."

Judith nearly looked behind her, but she did not want to

give away that she had heard a noise. Perhaps it was nothing. Or worse, it could be a poacher or someone less eager to help her. "You should not leave it," she said. "If you are so committed to your cause, stand and defend it."

Tattershall laughed bitterly. "Let the English execute me for believing in the betterment of mankind, for standing behind our emperor? I shall do no such thing. And I will laugh when you hear of my victories, when you have to improve your French to exist in our empire. Your accent, by the way, is atrocious. Almost as bad as your friend's."

The sound came, and both Tattershall and Judith turned. Two dogs ran towards them, barking loudly, dashing after them with great speed. A man and a woman followed them on horseback.

"Stay where you are, and don't think of moving." Louisa-Margaretta pulled her mare to a stop. "I'm sure you don't need me to say it in French."

❧ 46 ❧

They had planned to leave early, but there was some trouble with the trunks. The elder Mrs Haddington had decided that the younger must take more fine clothing than she would have desired for herself, even in her undisturbed hours.

Judith stood only with her father. She had wanted to speak with Miriam about her task, but Miriam was careful to stay at a distance from them both. "Get thee to a nunnery" had been an order, and nobody in her family yet knew how closely Judith meant to follow it. Perhaps once Miriam understood that Judith was serious in her intentions, she would not be quite so silent. If both Louisa-Margaretta and Miriam were not speaking to Judith, the wait was bound to be a lonely one, no matter how much Judith felt that she deserved such a punishment.

Her father would have objected. Even as he stood beside her, warm in his woolen cassock, he kept reminding her that he wanted her to stay in Brackenfield. Since summer had come, he had argued for the better part of a week. It was really a rather pleasant place.

"It will feel more like a home in time," he said. "And when your aunt arrives—"

"My aunt is coming for Miriam, Papa," Judith said, her voice near breaking. She tried to keep herself from the thought of staying and surrendering to her aunt's wisdom and interference.

Next to her, Peggy Haddington shivered in the sun. Her eyes were turned to the horses but unseeing.

"I am needed elsewhere." Judith attempted to smile. "My task is my own."

"'I struck the board and cried, "No more! I will abroad,"'" her father quoted.

"Haven't you always held that George Herbert's poetry was heretical?"

He smiled. "The more I live, the more I understand the man's views on his calling, even if I think his expression of them rather dramatic. I like to think I do not go on about heresy as much as other vicars."

"But you are a rector now."

"That is true, my dear. And perhaps that is the point. I have learned a great deal in the intervening years."

Silence followed, and Judith lowered her voice. "Papa, perhaps you understand, then. I do not want to stay here, not with all the memories."

"Was that not Mr Herbert's point, my dear? The memories will accompany you."

Judith reflect on that. Tattershall, or rather Mrs Oakley, had been captured. Loyal to Napoleon Bonaparte to the last, she had refused to provide information on anyone else, but she had made it clear that she was the one who had killed her husband. Though it would have been a great scandal, the army managed to keep it rather quiet, as they did not like to admit how they were caught out. Two of their own had agreed to a duel, then another had been falsely accused of murder and very nearly hanged. The story did not reflected well on anyone.

The carriage was loaded, and for a moment, she was caught up in the embraces of all the party.

Mrs Haddington, in particular, had tears in her eyes as she blessed the journey. "You are a blessing in every sense of the word, dearest Judith. I cannot tell you how much it means to me that you shall be watching over Louisa-Margaretta and Peggy on this journey. I wrote directly to Cousin Morgan this morning, and he has been helping with all the arrangements."

Words stuck in Judith's throat. On hearing the name, she had a great deal of questions. *Will I encounter the man I rejected only months ago? Will he be solicitous for another's sake, or will he wish to see me settled as well? What will he make of my rash decision to accompany Peggy to the only madhouse in England where she will be well looked after?*

Mrs Haddington had moved on to her daughter, and her voice was much more terse than usual. "Louisa-Margaretta, dear. You will write to us, won't you? And know that you can always return?"

The response was clipped. "I will not return to Wycliff Castle, but if you like, I will write."

"A fine concession from a daughter."

"Even you saw that I was never happy here. And this is the most respectable way to go off to a friend whose company will not raise a single eyebrow."

"Mrs Haddington's voice went from stone to sorrow in ͜nt. "But will you be happy there, my dearest?"

͜etta shook her mother off. "I do not know. ͜ill not be a prisoner."

͜led along, Judith kept the window ͜pa and the Haddingtons until she was ͜f sight. It was long before they were out of the park. After all, the Wycliff Castle grounds were extensive.

"Louisa-Margaretta," Judith said quietly, seeing as Peggy was asleep.

It was as if the broken woman were a sleeping child, and they had to whisper around her.

"Louisa-Margaretta. Please." When Judith received no reply, she could not help but sigh. "It is too many miles. How are we to make the journey go any faster if we cannot speak?"

"Perhaps we ought not to say things we may regret," Louisa-Margaretta snapped, and Judith shifted in her seat.

Mrs Peggy Haddington leaned against her, which was not at all comfortable. Louisa-Margaretta had her side all to herself.

"I do regret what I said," Judith told her. "And I am sorry."

"That is something, I suppose."

"Also, I think you should not go to your friend in London."

Louisa-Margaretta glared at Judith, forgetting to whisper. "You think I am mad to marry for money and a position. Well, I think you are mad to go to a madhouse. Who says you will not come out worse than Peggy? You would have been better to stay in Brackenfield and brave things with your sister, not flee out of cowardice."

Judith burned with fury. "I am not being cowardly. I am staying with a woman who is in greater need! Your sister, in fact."

They both looked at Peggy Haddington. She was a kind woman who had suffered a great deal, but both knew she did not feel like a sister. Louisa-Margaretta and Judith had more of the regard, and perhaps even more similarity of spir‍ found in true sisters. More of the anger too.

Louisa-Margaretta's voice was harsh when she ans‍

"You go there, then, Judith, and I can say that I do not wish madness upon you. But you would do well to stop speaking ill of my plans. If that means we cannot speak, so be it."

Mrs Peggy Haddington stirred, and Judith fought back tears as she tended to her. She had lost both Miriam and Louisa-Margaretta, and if she was not careful, she would lose Peggy to another force.

Louisa-Margaretta sat aloof across from her, picking at her bonnet, no doubt trying to arrange it in a style that would pass the strict scrutiny she would encounter in town.

Without speaking, she said a prayer for all three of them. The next season of their lives began with a long journey, and she could not say where any of them would end up at the journey's end.

ABOUT THE AUTHOR

Eve Tarrington is a Jane Austen fanatic. She has written dozens of books, but this is her first historical mystery set in the Regency era. She is thankful to her readers, her family, and her friends.

Would you like to know when Eve Tarrington is putting out a new novel? You're in luck! Join the mailing list at tena ciousteacuppress.com/eveTnews. You'll get an email when a new book is coming out.